THIS ISN'T THE PLACE

A COLLECTION OF UTAH HORROR

Timber Ghost Press

This Isn't the Place: A Collection of Utah Horror

Copyright © 2024

Published by Timber Ghost Press

Printed in the United States of America

Edited by: Beverly Bernard

Cover Art and Design by: Don Noble

Interior Design: Timber Ghost Press

Print ISBN: 979-8-9883040-7-4

www.TimberGhostPress.com

CONTENTS

FOREWORD

T.J. Tranchell

P ioneer Day

I have long argued that a ghost need not be present for a haunting to occur. As it turns out, a home—a house—is also not required.

As I write this, it is Pioneer Day in Utah. Like other states celebrate statehood anniversaries, Utah celebrates the day the Mormon pioneers first entered the Salt Lake Valley. The legend is that prophet Brigham Young declared, "This is the place" upon seeing the valley. That statement has haunted the area ever since.

The summer day is hot and bright and fireworks will blight the night skies across the state and into neighboring Mormon towns in Nevada, Idaho, Colorado, and Wyoming. The bangs startle pets and vets, and children allowed to stay awake past school year bedtimes will crawl beneath their beds. Sleepless nights will plague many residents. Not all hauntings are quiet.

And not all hauntings are indoors. Hiking trails, which abound in Utah's natural beauty, can be haunted. Groves of trees, a familiar setting to any Mormon, have their ghosts, too. Such places remind us of folk horror and gothic tales, the old dark woods where monsters dwell. Those old stories, even told new, resonate for a reason.

Speaking of gothics, prisons and cemeteries are ripe for a variety of hauntings. The Utah State Prison has its share of ghosts, some more famous than others. Known as Point of the Mountain, the prison complex was recently demolished. But as we know, just because you move a building doesn't mean you've relocated the specters of the past.

We do all too often expect our haunted places to be old and derelict. Train stations, hotels, hospitals, and unused asylums are ghostly breeding grounds. Yet there is excitement in the possibility of more modern places being touched by entities from beyond the grave. Gun ranges and Wal-Mart get some time in this volume.

But still...

Stop me if you've heard this one. A family moves into a new home. It is supposed to be a safe place. Four walls and a roof—a refuge from the outside world. I know you've heard it and I admit that I am working on a novel with just such a premise. (Yes it is set in Utah because Utah is a place that haunts me.) The houses in these stories, though, don't differ that much. Maybe they are isolated or have some tragic backstory. None of that matters because this isn't about a place as much as it is about people. No one cares about the abandoned theater (okay, I do but that's a different story) until someone decides to cross its threshold and peel back the curtains again. It is all about people. All of the stories here have interesting people, some of whom get a degree of comeuppance and some we hope escape as untraumatized as possible. What makes a ghost story ring out like Pioneer Day fireworks isn't where it happens but who it happens to.

Utah is a haunted place, as much as New England or the South. This group of writers proves, again, it isn't as much about the place as it is about the people. Some other white people would have eventually settled the land that became Utah, spilled as much indigenous blood doing it, and moved on with their lives. But the Mormons are the ones who did and their specter continues to cover the state in almost all areas of life and death.

So kick back with your favorite nonalcoholic, caffeine-free beverage, and prepare to be haunted, wherever you might be.

T.J. Tranchell

Pioneer Day

July 24, 2024

"My Best Friend"

Steve Capone Jr.

If I could silence her with a pillow, I might finally get some shuteye. But it never worked when I was a kid, and it's not working now. She's got a firm grip on my mind, but that doesn't stop me from trying. I press harder, distending the pillow like a finger in a car door, wishing I could shut her up. She's in my mind but not of my mind, not a figment of my imagination. She has a will separate from my own and follows her wishes, which only occasionally align with my own. She's not a typical imaginary friend, birthed from someplace in my mind. And despite the fact that she's not something I thought up, she filters through my cushiony bastion like blood through a colander. Some best friend, right?

Katie is here for me, which again spells trouble for everyone else. Mia and Ella have to get away from me, to leave—but figuring how I'll convince them they're not safe with me has stopped me from mentioning Katie's return. It feels too late to tell one and too early to tell the other. I've been here before, wishing Katie away and worried for those around me, but covering my head with a smooshed pillow won't make her go away any more than ducking underwater.

I've tried it with pool water, bath water, and lake water. I'd dunk and hold my breath, willing myself to believe she's gone while repeating a mantra, "Go away. Go away." I'd open my eyes, and she'd be closer than before, twelve inches from my nose, staring hard and grinning that bone-piano grin. Even expecting it, I'd freeze like a victim in a campy 80s slasher pic.

She doesn't go away.

If she gets hold of my wife, or worse, our child, they'll be paying for my cowardice—my lack of a spine. She's got to be back because of me and my choices, not theirs.

Katie's eyes are crystalline blue, her skin a terra cotta hue, her hair a darker shade of brown. Whether she's floating over my bathtub or beside me two feet under a swimming pool's surface, her hair doesn't shift or change appearance. It's always perfectly straight, bearing not a hint of reflected light. It's odd putting words to it, but this was one of the more upsetting aspects of Katie's way of being in the world. And my way of being in the world has ever been to indulge her, except for once, and for that, she taught me a lesson.

She's telling jokes again, and I'm nearly ready to admit defeat, to play her game, to do whatever she wants. I wrap both arms around the bamboo-stuffed pillow and wish I could blot my best friend out of mind as well as out of sight. Of course, I can't.

"Please stop," I mouth. I don't want to wake Mia. I know Katie understands, whether or not I speak the words aloud. She always knows what I want, but doing what I want is another matter.

"The aristocrats!" Katie says, finishing her joke. She beams.

I don't laugh, though I probably should. The proper reaction might satisfy her. But the joke isn't funny. It's disgusting, however she tells it, and my indulgences waver after midnight on work nights.

Katie began the endless variations of the joke soon after appearing in Elby's Woods, and she kept on telling that same joke, year after year. Last month, when she reappeared for the first time since high school,

I learned that some things don't change, even when they take a forced hiatus.

I've heard imaginary friends are some children's way of dealing with loneliness or feeding their creativity. I've always figured I exist more in the "I'm lonely" camp than living in creativity city, seeing as I wasn't much for artistic ventures and never had real playmates. None of my real-life acquaintances wanted to play the games I most loved.

Maze, for instance. It's kind of like the hot and cold game, but one player blindfolds himself while another guides him with hints. That, and it's only played in the aspen grove at the heart of Elby's Woods. The setting was key to the game's sepulchral mystique.

Things in the tightly packed center of the grove were confusing enough without blindness, but with it, escape without a guide becomes downright impossible. A blindfolded kid could walk for thirty minutes, seemingly in the same direction, and not find the edge of the core. If you could see and were to follow a compass, though, you'd be out in eight or nine minutes tops. Of course, the woods weren't actually infinitely deep. I found amusement in navigating ventricles arranged in what seemed to blindfolded me to be never-ending, ever-shifting quadrants.

No one but me seemed to be comforted by the deadly silence, the endless sameness of the place. It's not that I didn't feel the same fear as other kids. The fear captured me, too, but it held me fast, entrancing me when others had fled.

After a while, when it seemed obvious no one wanted to play Maze with me anymore, I began working out ways to play on my own. Katie showed up just then, friendly as anyone I'd ever met, and focused on entertaining me. She gifted me what I'd wished for from my other friends, but Katie did it better. She was mine, and I was hers.

Before too long, I didn't need anyone else. When I asked where she came from, she told me that she was called by my need, that I had been let be for too long, and in any case, her old best friend wasn't amusing anymore. But now we could entertain each other, playing Maze all day and Hunker Down at night.

Hunker Down, like Maze, was a game no one else wanted to play with me. I'd invented it, but Katie raised the stakes. To play well, you had to be able to stay hidden and quiet, and you had to hold still for hours. Katie liked to hunt at night, for which her perceptions were honed. If I wanted to avoid detection, I'd need to hide really well.

I started out hiding under my bed, but she discovered me pretty quickly and I had to find a new spot. The first time, she chased me around the house, shouting, "I'm gonna eat you up!" until my father found me hollering and tramping around. He sent me back to bed with a sharp word, threatening to throw me in "the hole," which I knew meant being grounded to my room, though he referred, half-joking, to an inhumane prison treatment that I had no business worrying about at that age. That was the last time Katie chased me during Hunker Down. Neither of us wanted to have to quit it entirely.

In later iterations of the game, I'd bury myself in the closet under my laundry and extra bedding and fall asleep. She almost never woke me, even after she found my second hiding place. There was no other good place to hunker, and Katie had always been considerate about things like that. Sure, she wanted me to entertain her, but she didn't want to spoil my fun—she wanted me to keep playing, after all. Despite her threats, she never ate me up, obviously. I'd be a pretty useless playmate if I were digested or got in too much trouble.

And of course, she was never dangerous to me. The people around me, though, while they had no certain reason as to why, considered me a parasite, leeching their sanity and good feelings, replacing them with confusion and awful sickness of spirit.

If I could get Katie to stop with the raunchy jokes, she'd probably want to play Hunker Down right now. She never tires. I'd forgotten this about her. But I can't play like I used to, on into the night. I need sleep. I haven't gotten a good night's rest since she came back to me.

I'd been sitting alone in a one-room movie house taking in a lunchtime movie, a regurgitated action flick no one wanted. During the climactic scene in which the jet-propelled helicopter crashes into the Wasatch Range mountainside, she grabbed me from behind. Even given her eighteen-year absence, I knew those hands—so damned cold.

In that instant, knowing the terrible feel of her hands didn't stop me from yelping, and I was grateful no one was around to hear me. I never liked her grabbing at my throat the way she did. I'd even gotten her to stop doing it before I'd sent her away to haunt someone else. Now, at the time of her triumphant return, she announced herself with a touch of the irascibility I believed I'd coaxed out of her. She must have been bored again. Or I called to her. I have to be rid of her again before she drives Mia and Ella both insane. Or before I lose my mind from anticipatory guilt.

And now, in bed, I feel those hands wrap around my wrists. Her skin is rough as though calloused from digging in the yard before showing herself after dinner.

I shoved her away, throwing off the pillow and miming, "Get!" because a real friend would let me be.

"Fine," she said, a dead frog perpetually in her throat.

I turn over and press my face into the mattress. She ceases to pester me, and I wonder if she'll let me finally sleep. What kind of playmate will I be if I wreck my car from exhaustion, or if I can't stay awake during daytime games? She might even convince me to return to Elby's Woods for a round of Maze, but not if I'm dead of exhaustion.

Katie doesn't have a lever for moderation—just an on/off switch. During my freshman year of high school, I learned she'd never stop on her own accord. I'd have to dispel her and take steps to ensure her absence. I'd gotten the idea of what to do from a movie about a grownup with a pesky imaginary friend. *Drop Dead Fred*, it was called. Only in that movie, the protagonist's best friend was a mischief maker, not anything truly dangerous. It was comedy, not horror.

Katie wanted to play with me, entertain me, and she didn't want to share. She was jealous. "Just the two of us" was how she wanted it. The arrangement suited me at first, but after several failed friendships destroyed in mutual incomprehension on the part of me and potential friend, I realized that as long as she was around, I'd have a tough time making a go of other friendships. And even if I could somehow talk someone through the visions flooding their mind, those people would never be safe around me. Around Katie.

There was no mystery as to where she'd go when she wasn't schmoozing me with her puns and dirty jokes. She'd tell me about her excursions afterward, as though I were a cuckolded husband, though it turned out I was the cuckoo, my own brood parasite laying eggs in the minds of potential friends.

Once Katie got into their heads, they couldn't be around me anymore. They'd run off, sometimes literally. When I got one of these victims—and victims they were—to admit what was bothering him before he ghosted, he'd gotten a sour look on his face. He explained that, whenever I was around, he'd see his little brother, eyes pulverized and leaking out of his head. He described this in a voice flattened as though he were dissociating, too terrified to approach even recalling the hint of a memory of what he'd seen. There'd been more gruesome visions, too, pouring through a spillway seemingly designed to upset.

Those who saw the visions hadn't themselves seen Katie. In fact, if they'd been able to see her at all, she'd warned me, that meant she'd selected them over me as playmate, and I'd lose her forever. Then the visions would be mine to behold. This explains why the kid I was warming up to in ninth grade switched out of Ms. K's third-period English class.

So, that's what she does. She ruins the minds of those around her best friend. In so doing, she is ruining my life. I don't know what would be worse: Katie poisoning my thoughts because she's imprinted on my wife or child, or Katie triggering grotesque visions of gore in their minds. Either one would be my fault, and neither would be sustainable. I've been staying away more and more, but I need to admit the situation is untenable. Mia and Ella's dreams have gotten so bad that none of us are sleeping much anymore, and I know why. I have to get rid of Katie again. I have to get my life back. But the cost...

Eventually, I grew fed up with Katie's antics, and I told another acquaintance about my possessive best friend. I don't know why I chose Peter. He seemed sympathetic, I suppose, and he'd said something in class about being interested in those absurd ghost-hunting reality TV shows. So, I picked him. He wasn't yet my friend, so maybe he'd be protected. That is, unless we failed banish Katie.

I told Peter that Katie wouldn't let me be and I needed his help, citing what he'd said about ghosts. I can't say why he took me at my word, and I have no earthly idea why he was willing to help. In any case, we decided we'd exorcize Katie from my life, but we didn't want to transfer her to someone else. She needed to be gone. Besides, if I couldn't have her, no one should.

We'd need to perform some sort of exorcism, but seeing as we weren't Catholics and had no other religion, we'd found a suitably non-denominational ritual online. We would need to say the words and burn some personal trinkets as token sacrifices.

This is where things went from bad to worse. The ritual worked, sure, but the trinkets weren't enough of a sacrifice. Katie exacted the balance due from my new friend, Peter, whose name I'll remember.

Just as he left my parents' apartment on Fourth, I saw Peter freeze at the edge of the sidewalk. I wondered what he was waiting for since his building was a few blocks north on the same side of the street. Half a moment later, he stepped in front of a city bus. I saw Katie for an instant then, standing over him, shaking her head. "I'm not mad, I'm disappointed," she seemed to be saying. When Peter gurgled his last breath, Katie disappeared.

Since the day my one-day friend sacrificed himself, I've forged plenty of relationships, and I've been careful to the point of obsession over the years not to call her back. I don't know the precise thing that triggered her arrival in third grade in Elby's Woods, but I believe it had something to do with a deep yearning to end my loneliness, a sincere wish not to be ignored anymore.

So, why is she back? Maybe I let down my guard. I'm married now, so I should be more fulfilled and far less lonely than when she appeared when I was nine. When baby Ella was born, her beautiful eyes captured my heart in an instant, and I lost most of my wife's attention.

Now, six years later and entering Mia's and my lucky eleventh year of marriage, I might have responded to my growing sense of abandonment by backing away—kind of a "You can't fire me—I quit" scenario. I've lately taken to going into the office on weekends, entertaining myself at other times bowling, seeing new releases at Harold's Moving

Picture House, or day drinking on the office couch watching baseball reruns. Lonely by choice, my therapist says.

Lying in bed, I realize while I've been reminiscing on my mistakes, Katie is gone for the moment. Maybe she'll allow me to steal badly needed sleep.

"I don't want to play." The voice echoes quietly from down the hall.

If my daughter is speaking to Katie, that means she can see her. That Katie isn't just tormenting her, laying eggs in her mind. In a flash, I'm out of bed, tears in my eyes. I practically fall into my daughter's bedroom, coppery taste in my mouth.

I manage to speak. "Who're you talking to, chipmunk?" I'm glad that in darkness she can't see my tears. I wipe them from my cheeks and the sweat from my brow.

Ella giggles. "My new friend. She wants to play with me."

I don't see Katie anywhere. Responding to the air in the room, maybe, I begin trembling. This isn't a figure of speech—I begin to shiver. A cold feeling overtakes me, and my compulsion at this moment is to get as far from my daughter as my legs will allow. The child in the twin bed in front of me begins to scream, her body growing like a bag of popcorn in a microwave. This is a vision. It isn't real. Katie won't hurt her. But Ella's new best friend will certainly hurt Mia and me, and it will be my fault. I have to get away. Ella's screaming stops, and that is somehow worse. I turn and run.

"The Discovery of La Santa Maria and What Came After"

Derek Hutchins

He was going to kill her. As soon as they found the treasure, he was going to stick a harpoon in her back, and Giovanna Leone would be shark food. Rowley had been searching for *La Santa Maria*, an exploratory barque that had disappeared off the coast of the Cook Islands, his entire life. In 1875, the ship had reported discovering vast amounts of wealth on the unexplored isle of Carmen del Rey and was heading back to a Spanish base in the Philippines when they sent out an SOS, which simply stated a single, haunting message: MUTINY. The ship was never seen or heard from again, and the treasure was never recovered.

Oh, many had tried of course, and many had become lost in their attempts. Rowley had led four expeditions for the lost vessel over the years, but this time would be different. With the aid of new technology, a remotely-operated underwater vehicle, or ROV, armed with advanced sonar capabilities, he had managed to detect the remains of a ship that resembled La Santa Maria in every regard, tucked away beneath an overhang at the bottom of a hidden trench.

Now, six months later, here he was, walking along the bottom of the aforementioned trench along the sandy ocean floor, staring at the back of Leone, a former Italian beauty, whose lust had veered from men to treasure. Her partnership had been necessary. Though Rowley owned plenty of diving equipment himself, he did not own a boat, or funds, to complete the venture, and his previous failed attempts had soured his reputation among his pool of investors. So, he had bitten the bullet and signed a contract with Leone, and though they were lifelong competitors, they had agreed to bury the hatchet and work together, just this once. He would share the location, and she would fund their venture and provide the boat and equipment. The contract was rife with litigation, stipulating legal regulations, and clarifying the nomenclature that any found riches be split evenly among both of them. Nomenclature which Rowley did not intend to honor.

He had devoted his life to finding La Santa Maria. It was not fair that Leone's greedy ass would take half of that away. As soon as the expedition plans had been finalized, Rowley had begun forming his own plans of how he would do away with her.

It was simple, really. They were alone in the middle of nowhere, hundreds of feet below the surface. Killing her was the only option, and no one would ever know. Once they found the treasure, of course. This was all hypothetical.

But his finger twitched on the trigger of the mini speargun he carried at his side, ready to fire at a moment's notice. The boat captain, Malone, a half-blind veteran from Utah and the third and final member of their team, did not question Rowley's decision to carry the weapon with him on his descent. It was in case of sharks, he had told them, and no one batted an eye. They were seven hundred feet below the surface, far deeper than most divers dared to go. For all he knew, they might run into Cthulhu down here.

Rowley allowed one gloved hand to trace along the cragged stone wall of the trench. His headlamp illuminated with sharp clarity the path directly in front of his face, but the space surrounding the ray of light was nothing but crushing blackness. It was a blackness like nothing he had ever experienced before, and he shivered, not from the cold, but from thinking of the sailors who had been pulled down to their unhallowed graves, trapped inside the hull of a sinking ship. *That way lies madness,* Rowley thought, forcing his mind to a different channel.

A safety line ran through a loop on his belt, connecting him and Leone to their diving bell a few dozen yards behind them. Diving this deep came with extreme risks. Commercial divers who worked on undersea structures would spend days or weeks in undersea housing to help them better adjust to the pressure. Rowley didn't have that kind of time. The diving bell was a metal transport hull, provided by Leone, that helped them get down to their desired depth and back up, making the adjustment to the pressure easier.

Rowley cast a glance behind, and to him, it seemed that the rope simply disappeared after a few feet. The diving bell was lost from sight. Reality was blurry this deep in the sea. For all he knew, he could be in outer space. He shook the foolish thoughts from his mind and focused on the task at hand. He placed one booted foot in front of the other, sending up ripples of sand that hung in the water, clouding his view. Leone was only a few feet in front of him, but she might as well have been a ghost, as all he could see was the general outline of her form. He could hear her breathing rhythmically through the piece in his ear. She had tried to strike up a conversation on the way down, but she had quickly learned that he wasn't one for small talk.

Rowley felt his foot connect with something solid. A rock? He used his boot to kick it upward and was surprised to find a modern scuba mask dancing before his eyes. He grabbed it and brought it closer for a clearer look. All kinds of debris ended up here, on the bottom of the ocean. Just because something had found its resting place here didn't mean anything... yet Rowley grew uneasy wondering if it was an omen. Perhaps someone had already found the ship and taken the treasure. He shook the thought from his mind, tossing the mask behind him. He couldn't think those thoughts.

The earpiece crackled, causing Rowley to flinch, as Leone spoke for the first time since touching down on the trench floor. "Okay, I think this is it."

Rowley's heart fluttered with excitement. He cast his headlamp around until it finally rested on the looming shape of the bottom of a wooden hull, several feet above their heads. The ship was jammed in between the two walls of the ravine, resting about ten feet off the ground. *What a resting place.*

Rowley kicked off the sand, paddling his legs with practiced motions against the restraint of his weight belt, to propel himself upward through the swarthy brine. He moved past a gaping hole in the ship's hull and didn't have to guess what had caused the vessel's demise. How the hole had got there was another mystery, one which he probably wouldn't solve today. He watched as Leone maneuvered through the opening, and part of him wanted to grab her leg and yank her back. How dare she enter first? What gave her the right? But he controlled himself and rested a hand reverently against the rotting, barnacle-encrusted wood. He pulled himself along the ship's hull, eyes searching for the sign that he desperately needed to verify this was the ship for which they were actually searching.

Then, miraculously, he saw it.

La...aria...

The rest of the paint had peeled, faded, or was covered with sea lichen, but there was no mistaking the evidence. He pulled a video camera from his pocket and filmed the image, proof more to himself than to the world, that he had found it at last. Not all the words were there, but they were searching in the right region, the ship was the correct size, and the words were clear enough that he could be sure this was it. A feeling of peace and triumph soared through him, but Rowley allowed it to dissipate, and a sense of dread took its place.

He had found the ship, but his enemy had beaten him inside. Rowley allowed himself to glide down, kicking with his legs, forcing himself toward the hole through which Leone had vanished when he heard his earpiece crackle again. "Rowley, I think you better get in here."

If he wasn't panicking already, he was then. *Keep it together, Rowley. Stay calm.* When you are down this deep, even the slightest elevation of heartbeat could cause you to burn through your oxygen supply. Men have died from even slight inconveniences like getting a foot caught for a minute or two. He had to make sure he was in control.

Rowley pulled himself through the hole, nearly ramming his face into a hatchet fish, which hurried around him. The space was cramped, but Rowley took a moment to appreciate the fact that this was a tomb, a place that no human had disturbed for over a hundred years. No one, until Leone. "Where are you? I'm inside."

"Keep heading back, you'll see me."

Rowley pulled himself through the black hole, catching glimpses of barrels and the remains of metal tools and silverware strewn across the decking. The floor was unstable, and he could see several holes poking through to the ocean sand bed below. During one of his strokes, Rowley's left hand caught on something in the dark (a piece of rope?), and something flew toward him out of the void.

Rowley screamed. He waved his hands back, flailing, then laughed as he saw what it was: a lichen-swallowed skeleton.

Breathing! Remember your breathing.

The body sank out of view, and Rowley took a deep breath to calm his racing heart.

"You all right?"

"Yeah," he replied. "Peachy."

Something caught his attention, and he looked up to see a ray of light up ahead at the end of a cramped hall. "See me?"

"Yeah."

Rowley pushed himself onward, joining up with Leone, and following her bloated form through a doorway. As soon as he was inside the chamber, Rowley gasped. Before them lay several barrels, one of which had burst open, Rowley guessed in the disaster that had sunk the ship, and spilled its contents all over the floor. The wooden boards beneath their feet were hidden beneath a cascade of gold. Coins, statues, crosses, and all manner of gold creations were among the haul. Many of the pieces were rusted or covered with lichen, but enough were clear that Rowley could distinguish their make.

Treasure.

The lost treasure of La Santa Maria. His at last.

Rowley reached his hand down and picked up one of the coins, twirling it between his gloved fingers. It was so rusted that he couldn't even see the markings, but still, it brought joy to his black heart.

"This is incredible," Leone said, and Rowley hardly heard her. He swam forward and used his knife to break open the lids of the remaining barrels. All of them were filled to the brim with gold or precious jewels. It was better than he'd ever imagined.

Holy Mary, we've hit the jackpot. Bermuda here I come.

Leone was inspecting the contents of one of the barrels. For several moments they were both stunned beyond words. Rowley cast his eyes over in her direction. Her back was to him. Now was the time to strike.

"They're never going to believe this." He heard the words in his ear, and they almost made him pause. There was so much treasure here, it might be possible to share after all. He could still backtrack...avoid the murders of Giovanna and Malone...

"They're never going to know." The words poured from his lips like they were always supposed to do. Rowley's finger pulled the trigger, sending the spear straight into Leone's gut.

He heard a muffled scream, and there was a flurry of bubbles that made it impossible to see anything in the murky deep. He saw the vague shape of Leone struggling, and he went for her with his knife, hoping to finish the job. His gloved fingers grasped her arm, but she squirmed out of his grasp, and he felt a hard kick delivered to his gut.

When Rowley shook off the pain, he saw the severed remnants of Leone's safety line drifting eerily in the ever-moving water. *Damn!* She was gone.

Rowley checked his oxygen meter. He had less than half a tank. He'd need to be careful. This tank needed to get him back to the bell or he was in deep trouble.

A trail of blood hung in the water, slowly dissipating like a cloud of smoke. He knew Leone was as good as dead. She was wounded hundreds of feet below the surface, she should be running out of air, and she had no safety line back to the bell. There was no way she would make it back up. But she could still make life difficult for him, and that blood would attract sharks...

Rowley gritted his teeth and swam out the doorway, following the trail of blood through the labyrinthine passageways. He could still hear Leone's staggered breathing in his ear and realized she could hear him as well.

"Leoneeeee," he practically sang her name, hoping to scramble her already fragile ability to think. He would take whatever advantage he could. His life's work was on the line. "If I don't get you, the sharks will, Leone. Better to end it quick."

The trail was easy to follow. A crimson cloud led Rowley up a flight of collapsed stairs into the second level of the ship's bowels. He was in a larger space now, perhaps the mess hall. He was overtaken by the sudden feeling that he was being watched. Anxiety crept up inside his chest, squeezing his lungs with an iron fist. He swam fast through the open space, past a school of fish, and entered another cramped hall. The trail ended in the center of the passage. Adjacent to Rowley's position were three separate doorways, and there was no way to tell which one Leone had entered. *Damn it all to hell*. He could either man up and choose one, or wait, and if he waited, that might allow Leone more time to escape. There was no way to tell which of these doorways led to dead ends without exploring each of them. *Damn it all to hell a thousand times!*

Rowley chose the nearest door on his left. The room was a small space, barely six feet wide. A storage room of some kind, he guessed. He caught a quick glimpse of a standard diving dress, the old kind that folk aboard this very ship might have used, back in the early days of scuba diving. But it was clear Leone was not there.

As Rowley explored the room, he saw a flicker of movement out of the corner of his eye. For some reason, the words Leone had said to him on the journey down echoed in his mind. *This ship is cursed*. She'd said it as a grim joke, but he couldn't help but wonder now if there was some truth to them. However, as he turned, all he saw was the diving suit, drifting strangely in the ever-shifting waters.

Rowley backtracked into the hall, eager to get out of that room, and as he exited the door, he felt something hard crack him on the skull. His vision went dark for a moment, and he heard something heavy clunk against the sagging wood below. In the quick glance he caught of the object, it looked like a cannonball.

Leone was on him instantly. She had used the object to disorient him so she could make her move. *She has no idea who she's dealing with*, Rowley tittered internally. *She's stepped into the lion's lair*. Rowley saw Leone swinging her knife at him and caught her wrist without much effort. He was by far her physical superior. She kicked and struggled, but he was able to spin her around, holding her by her oxygen tank, and in one swift flick of his wrist, he severed her oxygen line.

Leone floundered in the water, and for one second, Rowley caught a glimpse of her panicked eyes through her goggles as she guzzled water. He moved back and watched, not because he wanted to, but because he had to be sure she was gone. He had to be sure she was dead. That was the only way he could be safe. Leone quickly realized what had happened and slid the oxygen tank from off around her shoulders, confirming her fate. She thrust a middle finger at him before using her remaining strength to jab her blade in his direction, an action which Rowley just managed to avoid before he stripped the knife from her hand. *Poor girl*. She was out of options, so she had tried her only remaining hope: to get Rowley's tank. It wasn't going to happen.

Within two minutes, she had stopped moving and was nothing more than a floating corpse inside a haunted underwater tomb. *Another soul for Davy Jones*. Rowley watched her for a moment. She was gone, so why did he still feel like he was being watched? He shivered and did his best to ignore the feeling. He checked his oxygen.

Quarter of a tank. He was running out of time.

Rowley left Leone there, making his way back toward the treasure.

The hard part was done; now the work could begin. He would have to lug all that loot out to the diving bell.

He descended back to the lower level and turned round the bend. As he was swimming toward the storage room where he knew the treasure lay, he saw something that made his heart stop cold. Movement. His first thought was that the sharks had finally caught onto the blood trail, but as he neared the doorway, he knew that what he was looking at was not a fish. Whatever it was had retreated inside the treasure room.

Rowley cautiously turned his gaze across the threshold, revealing a figure in standard diving dress, the same one he had seen while searching for Leone only a few minutes ago. But how had it arrived here? He couldn't quite make out a face through the small, circular glass window in the large, metal helmet, but there was definitely a body inside filling the empty space.

The question now became, who the hell was it? It couldn't have been Leone. Was it Malone? Another diver who was threatening his treasure? Rowley was out of spears, but he knew immediately that whoever it was would have to join Leone. They were implicated in his dark deed. This ancient ship would be their grave.

Rowley had no means of communicating with the person, but he didn't have to. He had nothing to say. Right as Rowley was about to lunge forward with his knife, the unexpected happened. A powerful ray of white light burst forth from the helmet of the deep diving suit. Rowley shielded his eyes, blinded by the strength of the light. What splendor. What force. What majesty. Rowley had never seen light so pure and heavenly as the light he now faced. He withered to his knees, unable to stand before the god in front of him. The diving suit rose several feet, bringing its arms out to its sides as if it were suspended in midair. As if to say, *Behold! I am that I am!*

Rowley dropped his knife. The light was mesmerizing. He was able to stand it better now. As he gazed into the unimaginable whiteness and glory, he understood that this, *this* was the real treasure. This was all that mattered. This light. He would give all he had to possess it!

He didn't even feel the rusted blade that ran through his heart. If he had turned around, he would have seen a legion of dead sailors surrounding him, all their rotten faces exposed in the spectral light.

"Your Final Mission"

Alicia Hilton

When the executioner pumps poison into my veins, sheath your claws. Cheer with the mob that congregated outside the Utah State Correctional Facility in Salt Lake City. Make them believe that you are Earthlings. Make them believe that they are the mightiest monsters in the galaxy.

When the crowd disperses, seek out the human governor who doomed me to die for crashlanding on his planet. Morph to vapor form. Glide through the Kearns Mansion fence, past the tall limestone columns, and under the front door. Follow the noxious scent of megalomania and hypocrisy.

When the politician sipping bourbon in the study sets down his glass, morph into rat form. Dive into the governor's mouth and down his throat. Wriggling, clawing, your undulating fur stifling his screams.

When the lungs cease to pump, burrow deeper. Caress the heart. Tighter, tighter. Embrace the muscular organ with all the love you received from me.

When the bowels empty, claw through the ribcage. Morph back to vapor form. Fly from Salt Lake City to the Uinta-Wasatch-Cache National Forest—a liminal space optimal for our spores to germinate. Follow Brighton Lakes Trail, ascending past Dog Lake, past Lake

Mary, Lake Martha, and Lake Catherine, rising to the top of Sunset Peak.

When dawn's first light gilds the horizon, form a circle. Link hands, open your gills, and release spores. Germinate, germinate until your descendants outnumber *Homo sapiens*.

"THE WITCHING TREE"

Cygnus Perry

Grandpa dared us touch the tree,
and none of us believed him
when he told us it belonged to
the ghost of something grim.

We marched the rocky hillside
seeing nothing in the brush,
yet each of us stayed ready
to turn around and rush.

The Juniper grew closer
as hearts raced even faster,
and the evening aged darker
as a shout cried danger.

Then all us children darted
down the dry rock pathway,
sending shrieks of our terror
into the twilight gray.

No one ever saw the soul
that stalks and haunts the summit,
but we always have agreed
Something lived there in it.

"Mushroom Hunting"

Caryn Larrinaga

A pit formed in Martin's stomach as he made his way up the overgrown trail next to Barrow Creek. His companion, a wiry physics major named Lucas, hoisted his backpack higher onto his shoulders.

"You ever been up here before?" Lucas asked.

"No," Martin lied. "But I heard it's worth the hike. Something about this mountain makes for a really smooth trip."

As the sun set behind them, Martin followed the rough trail around a curve, savoring the fresh smell of the pines until his long gray curls caught in the leaves of a low-hanging branch. He ducked below it, and his back twinged. He hissed with pain.

Lucas eyed him. "You okay, dude?"

"I'm fine."

Martin knew what the kid was thinking. To Lucas's eyes, Martin looked every inch like the old geezers he'd made fun of as a young Deadhead following Jerry Garcia around the country. Growing old had seemed like a choice then, something only people who weren't brave enough to live life to the very fullest were foolish enough to do.

He knew better now.

The trail meandered up the hillside, kept company by the gurgling stream. The day's flies buzzed off to parts unknown for the evening, replaced immediately by mosquitos that zeroed in on the hikers. Martin paused and sprayed himself with repellant before offering the can to Lucas.

After another half mile, the trail dead-ended rather than crossing the creek. The waters were narrow enough to step over, but Martin hesitated, holding up one hand behind himself to signal Lucas to stop.

This was it. The deep breath before the plunge.

Martin had crossed the stream unprepared the first time, splashing through like a child. Today, he tried a slow, deliberate entrance, like easing toe-first into a very cold pool. He leaned back and edged his foot across the creek. A tingle crawled from his toes to his aching knees, through his thighs, and up his torso. He brought his head through last, shivering as the sensation tickled its way across his scalp. If he'd thought to bring a mirror, he was sure he would see his scraggly hair standing on end.

The trees were thinner here, opening into a clearing just big enough for a small camp. Martin walked to the center of the circular space, and a hush fell around him, muffling the sound of everything outside the circle. The humming of insects faded away, and the burbling of the stream vanished behind the soft rustle of the aspens. It would have been relaxing if not for the ever-present ripple of energy dancing across his skin.

Lucas tittered behind him. Martin turned to find the youth running his fingers up and down his arms as though he'd never experienced goosebumps before.

"It's like... electric," Lucas said. "What is it?"

"No idea."

Martin unslung his backpack. He eased himself onto the ground and unpacked his bag. Out came a cushy sleeping bag, a lantern, a sports bottle, a gallon of water, and an assortment of apples and other snacks. Last of all, he retrieved a small bag of *Psilocybe semilanceata*.

As instructed, Lucas had come similarly prepared. He made camp beside Martin in the middle of the clearing. Once they had gotten settled, Martin wrapped the dried mushrooms into an apricot-flavored Fruit Roll-Up and held it out to Lucas.

Lucas hesitated before taking the bulging burrito. "You're going to watch me, right?"

"That's what you're paying me for."

"You'll make sure I eat and drink and all that?"

Martin patted Lucas's back and shot him a wise smile. "Kid, I've been tripping on gnome homes since before you were born. You're in good hands."

Lucas nodded and ate the Fruit Roll-Up. Martin watched him, unsure if the kid could even get it down. He'd given Lucas eight grams, more than the heroic doses he gave himself when he needed to fully rewire his psyche, but his instincts told him that for this to work, he needed Lucas to truly touch the sky.

Odds were that Lucas would never know the difference.

The boy climbed into his sleeping bag to wait for the mushrooms to take hold. Martin sat beside him and watched the fading light of the setting sun drift up the tree trunks, sipping a homemade OJ-and-ginger stomach prep from his sports bottle.

Darkness overtook the forest. High above them, pieces of the full moon peeked through the aspen leaves.

The stillness broke when Lucas bolted upright and started retching. Martin watched him for a moment to make sure the kid was fully consumed by his nausea. Then, quietly, he removed a second bag of mushrooms from his pack. It was another heroic dose, but Martin was prepared and ready for the ride. He tossed the dried pieces into his mouth. The bitter taste coated his tongue, but he grinned as he chewed.

He was thirty minutes behind Lucas. That was ideal.

In this place, it was better to be second unto the breach.

Martin had been shroom-sitting for decades. He thought of himself as equal parts sherpa and shaman, guiding friends up the mountains in their minds to find true religion. There was nothing in the world like mushrooms. They could change someone's life—he'd seen it a dozen times, borne witness to the healing power and spiritual awakenings that only psilocybin could provide.

At first, he did it as a favor. Then, he found an online forum where beginners could post requests for psychedelic tour guides, and Martin found his calling. It was a good gig. A hundred bucks just to stay sober for a night and make sure some dumb college student didn't do anything to hurt themselves? Easy.

He never needed a sitter himself. He had enough years of shrooming under his belt to trip comfortably in any quiet setting. But he enjoyed having company on the magic bus, so on the nights he needed to touch the sky himself, he had invited his neighbor Henry along for a ride. They weren't close, but Henry was a solid hiker and a low-maintenance co-tripper.

When the two of them got together, they hiked through the desert and up the mountains, searching until the energy of a place felt conducive to completely immersing themselves in the world beyond sight and sound. After three or four times in the same spot, the magic faded, and the hunt began anew.

It was Henry who found the clearing. He'd been mushroom hunting, looking for puffballs and morels, when he stumbled into the space.

"Martin, man, you won't even believe it. The energy up there is wild, just wild. It'll never fade, I can feel it. You gotta come check it out."

They trekked the short hike the next week. When they reached the creek, Martin hopped in with both feet, intending to let the water run over his sandals for a quick jolt of cold. What he got instead was a jolt of electricity. He stumbled forward, swearing, and came to an unsteady halt beside Henry.

"What the hell was that?"

Henry turned his easy grin on him. "Told you, man. It's crazy up here. If we can feel it this strong now, think how it'll feel when we're untethered."

The two men set up camp. Henry unscrewed the top of his metal thermos and raised it in Martin's direction.

"To swimming in the great sea of the universe."

Martin lifted his water bottle of stomach prep and tapped it against the thermos. Both men drank.

"You going all out, then?" Martin asked Henry.

"Yeah. I need it. Lotta stuff to sort through. You?"

"Just need a little reset and a good show. Three grams is all."

Within half an hour, Henry was sitting cross-legged, head tipped back, staring at the moon through the branches. Martin chewed his mushrooms thoroughly, juicing them between his teeth and watching the woods until his mind began to bend.

Around him, the shadows danced left and right, growing and shrinking. They stretched long, like ghostly fingers creeping across the clearing to caress the edges of the sleeping bags. One snaked up Henry's side and curled around his waist. A low moan rose from the woods, vibrating the tree branches.

Henry stirred. "You okay, man?"

Martin stared, unblinking, at the shadows. He had neither the inclination nor the ability to look away. After a while, it occurred to him that he hadn't yet answered Henry's question.

"So far, so good. Just getting started."

"Okay," Henry said. "Just next time, you know, ask me before you hug me, and don't moan at a man without warning, alright?"

A shiver ran through Martin. "You heard that?"

"Yeah, man. I hear you. Now would you sit down? You're gonna freak me out, dancing all over the place like that."

"I am sitting down."

With a grunt, Henry propped himself up on an elbow. He twisted and faced Martin, and Martin caught a flash of confusion on Henry's face before his eyes went wide with awe.

"Angels," Henry breathed. "I always knew they were real."

Martin didn't turn around. He knew from experience that whatever Henry was seeing was in his own mind, and even if Martin looked at the same oddly shaped tree or glowing full moon, he would experience it in his own way. He was far more invested in watching the shadows.

A burst of energy sparked in the air behind Martin, singeing his long gray locks. The sharp odor of burning hair screamed for his attention. With difficulty, he pulled his gaze from the tendrils of shadow surrounding Henry and looked over his own shoulder.

Holy shit. He could see them.

They didn't look like angels. Not like the ones in his childhood Sunday school coloring book, and not like the many-eyed monsters he'd seen in a painting at an arts festival. Though they were barely more than shadows, something about their shape struck him as human.

Four forms slipped through the spaces between the trees. Their edges darkened, and Martin could make out the curves of their hips and the swells of their busts.

"They're women," he said. His voice echoed strangely off the trees, his words glowing crimson in the air. "Or... they were."

The sight of the spirits didn't frighten him. After the things he'd seen and the journeys his mind had taken, this sudden certainty of the supernatural didn't take him by surprise. Rather than fear, curiosity filled him. He wanted to ask Henry who he thought the women had been.

He never got the chance.

As Lucas's heaving subsided, he sucked in air, gagging on his own spit. His shoulders shook, but nothing came out of his mouth. Martin nodded approvingly. The kid knew how to follow instructions; he'd kept his stomach empty.

The thought made Martin chuckle, and he brushed aside his normal shroom-sitter tendencies. What did it really matter if the kid threw up?

He checked his watch. It wouldn't be long now. His own dose would hit soon. He stood and stepped mindfully around the rectangular indentation where Henry's sleeping bag had been just a few weeks before, brushing a scrap of yellow police tape with his toe as he re-packed everything he'd brought. After he strapped his rolled-up sleeping bag to his backpack, he settled onto the cool ground with the pack over his shoulders. When it happened, he'd be ready.

"I think it's starting," Lucas murmured. A soft cry escaped his lips, and he curled into his sleeping bag.

Not long after, Martin's mouth opened wide in an enormous yawn. His senses lifted out of his head and floated upward into the branches. Sound returned to the clearing, and the buzz of insects and the whisper of the breeze swelled in volume. He closed his eyes. Colors kaleidoscoped across the backs of his eyelids, the shapes shifting and folding in on one another as he slowly breathed in and out.

He could have stayed that way for hours, watching the colors until they sang, but that wasn't what he'd come here for. That wasn't enough, not anymore. He opened his eyes and focused on the tree line.

Henry's scream had torn through the clearing. Martin whipped his head around, and a sense of loss washed over him as he lost sight of the ghostly forms. The feeling was immediately replaced by horror as his eyes found his friend.

Gray shadows coiled around Henry's waist and lifted him off his sleeping bag. His body twisted unnaturally, and he spasmed in the air, legs jerking and head rolling. Through it all, a single, steady shriek poured out of his gaping mouth.

Martin stared in terror. He wanted to move. In his mind, he saw himself lunging forward through a wall of dripping pastel paint, grabbing Henry's legs, and yanking his friend to safety. But his feet refused to budge, glued to the ground by the sound of Henry's agony.

The scream abruptly cut off. Henry's body thudded to the ground.

The impact reverberated up Martin's legs and through his bones, unlocking his joints. His imagined heroics failed to manifest in the real world. He bolted out of the clearing and back across the stream. Unsteadily, through changing colors and unfamiliar shapes, he stumbled down the trail. Branches tore at his hair, ripping out clumps of shimmering strands. His knees burned. His back wailed. His aging, aching body protested every step. It begged him to slow down, told him this was nothing more than the first bad trip in over fifty years.

His mind disagreed.

He found safety in his van and rode out the rest of his trip there. By morning, he felt normal, but couldn't process what had happened for days. His stupor broke when he saw a news report about Henry's body being found in the woods by a hiker and her dog. Police attributed his death to a heart attack brought on by an extremely high dose of psilocybin. They put out a general call for the person who left their sleeping back and camping supplies in the forest to come forward and shed more light on the situation, promising that no charges would be filed. In his living room, Martin flexed his hands and studied his fingers, grateful he'd never been arrested. His prints were on that water bottle.

Feeling safe for the first time since he and Henry had sat down in that clearing, Martin turned to the difficult task of separating the reality of that night from the hallucinations. Henry had died. That much was obvious. But not from a heart attack.

A trace of paranoia whispered that maybe it had been a hallucination, or worse than that, a rare veer into psychosis. But the sounds of Henry's screams were carved onto Martin's eardrums, and that was real enough to allow him to brush away his skepticism and focus on the facts at hand.

First, Henry was dead. There was nothing he could do about that, and now that he no longer feared his own arrest, Martin had far more interest in the second fact:

The clearing above Barrow Creek was haunted.

Somehow, Henry had stumbled onto proof of an afterlife. Connected as the mushrooms had allowed Martin to be with the oneness of the universe, there was an entire other layer he was missing.

The thought ate at him. As weeks passed, the outlines of the four ghostly women burned in his retinas like the afterimage of an eclipse. He needed to know more about them, to fill in the blanks in his mind. Who were they? Where had they come from? And how could he bridge the gap between himself and this disconnected place?

Martin combed through the memories of that night. Henry had called the ghosts "angels." Had he seen details Martin hadn't? More than just shadows in the dark? Martin wanted to see what Henry had seen. But how could he do it without ending up like Henry? He chewed on the question, unable to find an answer.

Then Lucas posted on the forum, looking for a guide.

A low moan oozed into the clearing on the breeze. Lucas answered it with a moan of his own as the barest hints of shadows curled around his waist.

Martin held his breath.

They were coming.

Slowly, as the shadows thickened once more, the unearthly moan rose in pitch, strengthening into the clear tolling of bells, one tone at first, quickly separating into four distinct voices. The sounds became colors, and each vibrant shimmer of gold, purple, crimson, and blue settled atop a shadow like a crown. The colors dripped down the edges of the invisible forms, draping over soft curves like fine silk.

Joy filled him. Henry was right; the ghosts were so beautiful they could be angels. And maybe that's all an angel was—a spirit of such pure brilliance that she outshone the moon.

One of the high bells chimed again. The purple shade inclined her crown toward the men.

Martin exhaled slowly. This was it. No turning back now. The spirits knew they were here.

"Do you see them?" Lucas whispered. "Is this real?"

Martin said nothing. He couldn't be sure what Lucas was seeing. And for the boy's sake, he hoped Lucas couldn't see what was coming.

Breath by breath, the phantoms moved closer, floating across the dried grass without rustling a single blade. As the shadows crept toward Lucas, a curtain of darkness followed them. Martin raised himself into a half-crouch and backed away from the boy. The tickling sensation of the grass on his skin multiplied and zipped up and down his body. Each time he blinked, fractals of color burst to life behind his eyelids. His vision alternated between light and shadow, and he felt the electric tingle at the edge of the clearing on his fingertips as the four ghosts converged on Lucas's sleeping bag.

A shriek tore through the night.

Martin clapped his hands over his ears, but the sound had already wormed into his mind. It echoed backward and forward, inverting itself and slowing down like a melting record.

Light flashed. Martin winced but forced himself to keep his eyes open. He hadn't come all this way to miss the only moment that mattered.

As he watched, the women lifted Lucas into the air in one smooth motion. A yellow glow surrounded him. The shades nipped at the glow, tearing off bits and pieces. As they absorbed the edges of Lucas's spirit, their halos burned brighter, slicing a rift through the darkness above the boy's spasming body. The rift tugged at Lucas's soul, widening as it consumed him.

Martin leaned forward, desperate for a better view through the crack in the sky. He could see movement on the other side, gray shadows fluttering and pulsing in the haze. Too quickly, the last of Lucas disappeared through the slit, and it zipped closed into darkness as though it had never been there.

The four haloed shadows hovered above the boy's corpse. Their forms hardened at the edges. Martin blinked, and the shapes became tall figures, lithe and graceful.

One turned. Pale eyes opened.

She *saw* him. And in that instant, Martin realized he'd waited too long. The spirits had finished with Lucas and were ready for their next meal. As one, the four spirits rushed toward him.

Martin screamed. He rolled backward, tumbling out of the clearing and landing flat on his back in the shallow creek. Dripping and sweating, he wrenched himself to his feet.

Once more, fear propelled him down the mountain. He stumbled as he rounded the back of Lucas's car to his old GMC Vandura. Hands trembling, he yanked the door open and threw himself inside. He felt safer where a thick layer of American-made steel separated him from the spirits in the clearing.

When the peak passed and the mushroom's effects waned, he realized that all he'd done tonight was discover more questions to be answered. He had to know more. What he needed, he decided, was more time. A bigger buffer. Three or even four Lucases.

Martin climbed into the driver's seat and left the boy's car behind him. There was only one way to get a better view of the other side, and the shroom-sitter forum was only a click away.

"THE GHOST OF CHRISTMAS PRESENTS"

C. H. Lindsay

Martha hated Christmas. If she had her way, she'd hibernate from Thanksgiving to New Year. The worst part about the holiday was having to buy presents. It didn't matter how much she searched the internet and local shops, she always ended up at Wal-Mart for one vital last-minute gift. And the last place on earth she wanted to be—especially on Christmas Eve—was Wal-Mart.

It hadn't always been this bad, not before the incident in the toy aisle ten years ago. Each year since that night, she'd been forced to come back here for that one final purchase and always on Christmas Eve.

She hadn't come alone since then, either. She tried to get someone to come with her tonight, but everyone else was busy with family, and now it was after eleven and she had less than an hour before the store closed. Less than an hour before Christmas.

She looked to see if any toys had been put up front for last-minute shoppers, but there was nothing for a toddler. Not even a Christmas teddy bear. "Open 'til midnight but nothing up front?" she groused. Martha looked for a cashier to send back for a doll, but there were none in sight. "Great." She had no other option but to go to the toy aisle and hope they weren't expecting her this late.

She pushed her cart down the hardware aisle as it was the safest route and grabbed a wrench and a crowbar for protection. At the end of the aisle, she slowly looked left. Two aisles down, she noticed an army soldier peeking out from behind a wire container filled with rubber balls. As soon as he saw her, he pulled back. They were waiting for her.

She looked at the brightly colored balls for a long moment. No, she'd done that last year and it took six months before her sister would talk to her again. She then considered grabbing whatever was on the end of the aisle and running to the checkout stand, just in case she couldn't get what she came for.

She looked at the nearest shelf. Duct tape. Not a gift for a little girl. Her sister would be upset again if everyone else got something nice and Nancy got a roll of tie-dye duct tape. She'd be banned from family dinners if she did that. She rejected the idea of buying a box of cookies for the same reason.

Martha took a deep breath and pushed the cart around the corner. She might still grab the first practical gift and run for the checkout stand before they could get her.

As she reached the ball bin, she heard something flapping. Looking up, she caught a flash of a wing—or was it a tail? Another recon or aerial assault? She checked her watch. It didn't matter. She had twenty minutes to get a gift and get out. She grabbed several balls and dumped them on top of the tools.

One aisle from the toy section, Martha heard high-pitched whispering. She put her purse over her shoulder and set a ball in the kid seat as another weapon. She was going to need it.

She knew from talking to people online that the perfect doll was just down that aisle. A modern-day version of Betsy Wetsy. In addition, her sister strongly hinted that it was the one toy her daughter wanted. Martha had no idea why. It was a stupid toy then, and it was a stupid toy now.

The whispering grew to a hum. Martha threw the first ball over the top of the shelf, then grabbed more balls and rolled them down the aisle as decoys. She zipped up her jacket and pulled the hood down to cover as much of her head and face as she could. Then she threw the remaining balls, not caring what she hit. She heard thuds and curses as she ran around the corner. Nerf guns went off, hitting her with dozens of foam balls, but she only tightened the hood of her jacket and grabbed the crowbar.

A line of plastic soldiers formed halfway down the aisle. She wasn't sure what they thought they could do. They were no match for an angry woman with a shopping cart and a crowbar.

Collectible Barbies jumped from the top shelves; some fell into her cart, and some landed on the ground and tried to trip her. She'd use one of those if she couldn't get the Betsy Wetsy. Retro Cobra G. I. Joes climbed up her clothes, clawing their way to her face. She shook off as many as she could, then swung the crowbar wildly as she pulled off the rest, throwing them as far away as possible.

Several of the dolls in the cart tried to lift her wrench. "Oh, hell no!" Martha pushed the cart down the aisle, knocking over the army men. Served them right.

There was Betsy Wetsy, just ahead of her. It looked like she was issuing orders to the others, but Martha didn't hear any words, just a strange, raspy whispering. Enraged that the doll she wanted seemed to be inciting the others, Martha shouted, "You can't beat me! You're nothing but plastic!" She was determined to get that obnoxious doll now more than ever. There was no way she'd let these mini monsters win!

Figurines lined up behind the remaining army men, blocking half the aisle. Pocket monsters, micro cars, and superheroes filed in from the next aisle to join the fray. Above them, teddy bears reloaded their Nerf guns and continued shooting.

Several creatures began growling behind her. She knew she shouldn't, but she looked over her shoulder. Plush dogs, bears, cats, monkeys, and dinosaurs were filling the aisle. Panic climbed up her throat, tasting like the burrito she had for dinner. This had been a bad idea, but she was knee-deep in it now. "I will not let you win!" she shouted. Martha threw the crowbar at the superheroes, scattering them long enough for her to lunged for Betsy Wetsy. The doll bit her hand and she smacked the box against her leg, causing the doll to go quiet. Good. Now she just needed to figure out how to get to the checkout. She looked for a phone to ask for help, not sure if this store even had one, but she didn't see it. She turned back to the aisle behind her. The Barbies and Kens now joined the others, and the army men stood on the heads of baby dolls to take aim. The shelves around her now held mostly empty boxes.

There were fewer stuffed animals behind her than dolls in front. She held Betsy Wetsy like a football and jumped over the stuffed animals.

She was vaguely aware of a voice announcing that the store would close in ten minutes. Time was running out.

She turned left to go back to hardware, but the ball bin had moved and now blocked half the aisle. Skateboards filled the other half. She looked over her shoulder. That way was packed with a dozen bicycles, their streamers blowing in the breeze from the heating vents.

The incident in the toy aisle ten years ago played through her head. That night she was after one particular toy for her nephew. She couldn't remember what it was, but there had been one left, and a little boy was reaching for it. Martha pulled it out of his hands, knocking him to the ground. The kid could get another toy. He didn't need it as much as she did.

As she turned away and headed towards checkout, smug in her victory, a pale old woman stepped in front of her. "It's not yours," she said sweetly. "The boy had it first. Give it back or live to regret it."

"Sorry, granny. It's mine now." Martha hurried past the woman, then turned around as she heard her mutter something. "What did you say?"

The old woman looked at her for a long moment, the expression in her eyes sad. "I said, 'May you never get the one toy you need until you have a true change of heart.'"

"Right. You're crazy." Martha turned back towards the front of the store, but the woman's next words stopped her again.

"Crazy?" The old woman giggled. "No. But if you don't heed my words, the toys will get you."

Martha didn't believe her then, but right now, she almost did. She shook her head. No. She could not, would not, believe that this was real. It was the stress of the season and the suggestion the old lady put in her head. Nothing more. Once she got out of here, everything would be normal again. Just like before.

With renewed determination, Martha ran, dodging or jumping over toys. One arm held the doll close to her chest, the other protected her face. Nerf balls pelted her in waves. Toy helicopters and flying creatures dived at her. Stuffed animals bit at her ankles. Growling, Martha kicked one toy after another out of her way so she could jump over the convoy of skateboards. The bicycles, fortunately, couldn't get through the mayhem. Just ahead she could see the aisle that turned to the hardware section and freedom. Betsy Wetsy bit her again. Martha held the doll's nose and mouth shut. She wanted to rip off its head, but she had to think of her sister.

Three feet from hardware, the barrage slowed. She was going to win. They could only get her while she was in the toy area.

And then dozens of balls came at her, followed by another faire of helicopters and flying creatures. That, combined with a doll army on construction vehicles, was almost her undoing.

She spun, looking for a bat or other weapon to sweep them out of her way. A rubber snake wrapped around her ankle and tripped her. She righted herself, but then a drone flew into the side of her head, and she went down, landing on top of Betsy Wetsy. Just before she hit the ground, she thought she saw an old lady standing in the air above the toys, laughing.

All the toys began to pounce on her in a massive game of Dog-Pile and she lost consciousness.

The next afternoon when the employees opened the store, they found all the toys piled at the end of the hardware aisle. It wasn't until they had two-thirds of them put away that they found Martha's body. Something had hit her in the temple, leaving a large bruise and a trickle of blood. She was clutching a doll of an old woman in a Betsy Wetsy box. The doll was smiling.

"Folie à Plusieurs"

MJ Huntsgood

"What unfortunate soul is this?" I say to the creature, shriveled and seemingly quite miserable, clawing its way up the side of the slick stone wall. It laughs. The sound reverberates off of the dripping stalactites.

I have a vague recollection of an old radio show telling me that stalactites held tight against the ceiling and stalagmites might grow up to be a mountain. My colleagues tell me that they learned that from their mothers.

The creature laughs again. It has clearly been here a long time. I can't imagine it has showered in that time, and I'm no biologist, but I'm sure resting near this *thing*, no matter how much my feet hurt, could end up with me catching something.

I would have asked my guides about it if they had bothered to come this far into the cave with me.

It has taken six years to get this expedition funded. As the new head of the archeology department, it is my duty to make sure everything goes smoothly, but nothing is going right, not at all. After all, the supplies became rotten from a hole in the boat, and my guides were superstitious about this place.

"We have to wait until the lights go out," they said.

But I wouldn't wait. Not after this long.

I had enough supplies for eight days, a map, and torches. I could collect the data I needed to get our money's worth, I said.

Within twenty minutes, these things appeared. They were hollow-eyed and withered on the floors, sometimes laughing, usually just lying there.

I'm pretty sure they're alive.

I didn't scream, which is saying something, considering most of my colleagues think very little of my spine. Too hyper-focused. Head in the clouds.

I can't tell you how important this is though. This is my life's research. Everything I've wanted to know, it's in this cave. The ancient scrawlings from this period are said to have come from no culture, no era—but that can't be true. I have to push on.

I head over to the nearest wall, looking at the ancient lettering and rubbings. The photography equipment was destroyed, but I'm taking the best translations I can.

It's fascinating, like a rudimentary mathematical computer. I remember seeing things like this in science expos in London. Thousands of years old.

It is such a breakthrough. They'll give me enough money to send us back.

I need to stay here for more than eight days. I start to break my food in half and work on more rubbings. I have plenty of torches. I'll be fine. I need to learn what is in here.

I find the information is not just in words, they've actually drawn out a diagram that looks like tape, and a layout like the enigma machine. They've even designed something that looks like a chip.

I'm half a day in, and I have one day's worth of rations left when one of the *things* brings me bread. I don't know where it got it.

It knows.

It knows I'm close.

The *thing*, the thing wants me to find it.

I raise the bread, thank it, and get back to work.

It brings me bread every other day. My body gets used to the lack of food. The torches get dimmer, and I realize that I've long since run out of my own, and the *thing* gave me new ones.

I get used to the darkness.

I have to find out what I'm missing. What is the computer? What did it know? What is there? What is in the darkness?

The final torch is so dim. The light is so small. It gets dimmer. Dimmer.

It

Goes

Out

The darkness is oppressive. Like a smog that covers me completely. Utterly. I see all of the carvings on the wall light up in cool, warm blue. The deep, leather-like tightness of my skin fills in, and I feel warmth return to my muscles and the fat back to my body. I look around me, and the *things* stand up, their bodies turning back into people—tall and graceful, from all eras of the world.

"We thought you'd never turn out the lights," a man says, stepping over to me. He has honey-blonde curls and hands me a piece of bread.

"What happened?" I ask.

"Another's coming," he says. "You'll see."

I hear a voice coming down the hall. It's my assistant professor. "Six months! What could happen in six months?"

Torchlight fills the room, and the blue light from the carvings goes out. I feel the strength drop from my legs, and I sit down. My professor shines her torchlight on me.

"What unfortunate soul is this?" she says.

It's me, I try to say. *You always told me I had no spine.*

I laugh instead.

She'll find out soon enough.

We have to wait until the lights go out.

"Encore Performance"

Jonathan Reddoch

Scarlet Rose finished applying her last layer of five pounds of makeup. She was almost ready to take the stage to shake her sparkling tail feathers.

But as she approached the curtain, a tall, dark, masked stagehand stopped her. Erik whispered something inaudible and wouldn't let Scarlet pass. Scarlet kissed them and then pushed past to take the stage.

A live band played "Copa Cabana" from the shadows. The audience cheered in the darkened theater as Scarlet entertained them with "The Girl from Ipanema." Finally, after the last number, uproarious applause broke out.

The house lights were raised, revealing a standing ovation given by a congregation of charred corpses. Bony hands clapped into clouds of dust as scorched skulls shouted "Bravo!"

There they were center aisle: Teandra, Scarlet Rose's unhinged former lover, tear-stricken, blinded with jealous rage. Gas cans at their feet, they lit the handkerchief embroidered with the initials *SR*.

As the nightly encore performance, Teandra lit the theater ablaze. As they did every night.

"THE GRAVE HATH NO VICTORY"

Charles R. Bernard

For the third time in six months, a spotless white van pulled into the driveway of a Salt Lake Valley indoor range and gun shop. As it entered **COLD DEAD HANDS'** parking lot, it was directed by a uniformed police officer past yellow tape and into a spot behind the building, safely out of view of the main thoroughfare, at the owners' insistence. Willy Stewart, said proprietor, was concerned about the negative publicity from the most recent death by suicide on his range, especially considering that the act had been performed with a pistol and ammunition rented on the premises. The afternoon's events, he'd argued strenuously, had proved bad enough for business already. Thus, the van—towing a snow-colored trailer with **BIO KLEEN** stenciled on each side in arctic blue—complied and parked well out of sight.

In the van's warm, sterile-smelling interior, three men sat with the engine idling against the stagnant February chill. All were dressed in dark blue overalls and work boots. A stitched name patch sewn to each man's breast heralded them as Ephraim, Walter, and Holt. Walter Specht, sitting shotgun, bore a weathered baby-bald head. His face was rumpled as a field of clay above which his eyebrows held court like bushy white potentates. Holt Hansen, seated in the back, was seventeen years old and still in his first month on the job, a big deal for a high school kid. Holt was slightly moonfaced and kept his short hair neat. His frame was broad and burly as a bear and he, as Ephraim liked to joke, did all the heavy lifting—and all the heavy learning.

The last of the trio was Ephraim Allred, the driver. Like Walter, he was older, with a thinning ring of gray hair and honest, lean, clean-shaven features. Ephraim was the friendly face of **BIO KLEEN**, an avuncular bishop in the LDS Church and a passionate attendee of baptisms and ballgames alike. Chatty, choppy waters ran deep in Ephraim's case, as Walter knew. His longtime business partner's friendliness and gift for pleasantries masked a Mormon faith both deeply held and complex.

The three men waited for their client, contemplating the tableau of aftermath and wrap-up. They'd seen it nearly every time they'd gone to work. Eventually, Walter broke the silence.

"Four this year," he mused. "Three within the last four months."

Ephraim nodded warily. They'd been the company that'd handled the most recent triplet of suicides at the gun range. One woman and two men had followed the same pattern. A visit to the range to test the waters. **COLD DEAD HANDS** was not required by law to complete background checks before *renting* firearms; they merely had to verify a renter's age. They'd selected a weapon from the rental desk, carried it to the range, and used it to lethal effect.

"There's a darkness here," said Ephraim. He closed his eyes and shivered. "Will you all pray with me?"

Walter's laugh exploded in the van. This was evidently an old dispute between the two men, Holt reflected; Walter, who had left the fold of the Latter-Day Saints in the 1970s, and Ephraim, a devout (if dowdy) man who'd served an LDS mission in Peru, attended Brigham Young University, married, and produced a teeming brood of Allreds.

"I'm not going to pray with you, Ephraim," Walter said with an arctic smile. "As for the 'darkness' here, it's simple. Willy Stewart's harebrained libertarian ideas. *There's* all the darkness you need."

Ephraim frowned but took no umbrage. The argument was as long-running as their partnership; nearly as old, in fact, as their young trainee. Holt, for his part, wondered why they'd parked so far from **COLD DEAD HANDS'** front door. They had a lot to unload. Soon, two figures rounded the corner of the building: the thickset, sheepskin-jacketed Willy Stewart and a small, fierce woman clad in EMT scrubs and a reflective EMT jacket. Their conversation faded into audibility as they approached.

"...shut this fucking place *down* is what I think. How are you keeping this shit out of the papers?" the EMT snapped at Willy as he strolled toward the van. Ephraim, a shameless and inveterate eaves-dropper, peeled the window down to listen as the two approached.

"I will thank you *not* to take that tone with me, sister," Willy huffed.

"I'm not your fucking *sister*."

Willy treated her to a long-suffering sigh. "The paper *did* cover it," he said, referring to the LDS Church-owned Deseret News. "They ran that article about us just last month. About how hard these deaths have been on our staff."

Willy hustled up his pace, perhaps hoping to leave the persistent EMT in his dust. He hitched up his pants to facilitate this and, as he did, Walter could clearly see the rigid outline of a comically oversized handgun holstered near the shop owner's hip. A .50 Desert Eagle, or "Deagle," if Walter remembered correctly from their previous en-counters. The gun was more a badge of rootin' tootin' office to the shop's owner than a practical means of self-defense.

"You should be charged as a fucking *accessory*," spat the EMT. Walter could just make out her name on a plastic bade affixed to one pocket: PADILLA. He decided he quite liked Ms. Padilla.

"Well," huffed Willy as he reached the van, rapping one horny knuckle on the hood in greeting, "it's a good thing you ain't in charge. Now, I'd thank you to get the heck off my property before I have one of the boys in blue up there remove you." Pleased with this dismissal, Willy turned a sickly grin on Walter, Holt, and Ephraim. *Christ*, thought Walter with a thrill of palpable disgust, *he talks like he's in a squeaky-clean 1950s Western. What a horse's ass.*

"Cops are leaving," Willy said to Ephraim. "You guys can pull around front now. We've closed it up and the sign's turned off. Most of the lights, too. Brought your own halos, right?"

"Yessir," Ephraim confirmed. They had, indeed, brought halogen lamps.

Another EMT—this one a grizzled-looking fellow with a long, tan face—popped around the corner of the building and called Padilla's name. She clenched her fists, clearly contemplating one last shot at Willy Stewart, then stalked away.

Willy dropped a spare key into Ephraim's palm. The bishop got a good look at him as he did so. Beneath the bluster and the bullshit, Willy looked as though he hadn't slept well in months. It seemed like more than stress. There was real fear in those eyes, perhaps even terror.

"You boys have fun!" Willy said and then shambled off into the twilight winter smog.

Ephraim led the crew by virtue of seniority. He'd cut his teeth on crime scene and disaster cleanup before the field had been fully modernized and had endeared himself to entities ranging from the Salt Lake City Police Department to, evidently, Willy Stewart of **COLD DEAD HANDS**. If a city can be thought of as a human ecosystem, **BIO KLEEN** was a band of sextant beetles. Just as sextant beetles strip the flesh from dead animals and recycle it, the staff of Ephraim's firm turned death to profitable life. They helped reopen buildings ravaged by black mold, resuscitated drowned basements, cleared out hoarders' caches posthumously, and, of course, removed the residue of human death.

The three men gathered in the range where the self-injury had occurred: a long, concrete gullet of a room adjoining the gun rental area and, beyond that, the retail storefront. In Ephraim's experience, three things helped expunge the aftermath of death by suicide. The first was light, the second ventilation, and the third the right combination of chemical solvents. There were other requirements—elbow grease among them—and **BIO KLEEN** provided them all. In a way, they were fortunate to be working Willy's range again. The spacious range already came lit and ventilated, though not quite well enough for the job.

Some jobs were a brutal sensory assault. Here, the coroner had already carted the deceased away. The remaining cleanup would be less unpleasant thanks to the chill air inside the range. *Unusually chill, in fact*, thought Ephraim. Holt seemed to feel it, too. He rolled down both his sleeves to the wrist and stuffed his hands deep into his pocket. *It's not just me*, Ephraim noted with the evening's first touch of unease.

"It's as cold as a corpse's cock in here," said Walter, drawing a wince from Ephraim. "He ought to watch that," Walter added. He knelt and eyed a broad red puddle. "His pipes are gonna freeze."

"Hey!" Holt said with genuine good cheer, "My dad's a plumber! Maybe if we do a good job tonight and Elder Stewart's pipes *do* freeze..." He trailed off, realizing that both older men were staring at him with dry amusement.

"Let's get this carpet goin'," said Ephraim, grinning at Walter crookedly as if to say *this kid, huh?* "Get the carpet kit, Holt."

As Holt hustled to the toolbox to retrieve a prybar and clamps, Ephraim squatted next to Walter to examine their night's project more closely. *Not so bad*, he thought; a pool and some motley, mottled, red-and-black debris. The carpet was a mixed blessing: it had contained the mess at the cost of totaling the long strip of carpet that floored the stalls meant for each shooter on the range. It was a modest strip in a vivid green jewel tone. No great loss, really, in Ephraim's estimation.

The space between the range's shooter stalls and the targets was bare concrete, littered with glinting casings and bloated dust bunnies. At the terminal end of the range, the direction in which shots were intended to fly, a layered reception of sandbags, plywood, and cement languished in darkness. Above this narrow throat, a rail system ran outward from each stall. Shooters were expected to affix paper targets to the clamps that ran on these rails, send the targets yonder with the push of a button, begin a slow retrieve with another button, and then open fire as the sheets advanced. On **BIO KLEEN**'s previous jobs at **COLD DEAD HANDS**, the carpet had been left untouched by the fallout of suicide. Most of the range's floor was concrete. That was light work, though they'd had to remove some ceiling panels.

Holt returned from the toolbox with the prybar and carpet clamps, and the three men set to work.

A pair of 500-watt halogen light standups poured an unforgiving clarity onto the scene, and one of the team's dehumidifying fans had been set up and was hard at work and moaning loudly. Holt socked the prybar against the cheap molding, set the clamps, and—with help from Walter and a watchful eye from Ephraim—began to tear the strip up whole. It was the work of moments. The dusty, bright green carpet purred as it parted ways with the floor, revealing a long strip of much paler, cleaner concrete.

Cleaner with a notable exception, that was.

"What the heck is *that*?" Holt asked, his beetle-brow furrowing in genuine confusion.

"*That*," replied Walter in a contemplative tone, "is worth a phone call."

Walter, with his paralegal background, excused himself to call (and presumably berate) Willy Stewart. In his absence, Holt and Ephraim stood and stared at **COLD DEAD HANDS'** newly exposed scrap of concrete floor. Beneath the spot where the deceased had bled earlier that day, the concrete was dappled with a dab of bleed-through printed in the waffle pattern of the carpet's underside. What surprised them was the *other* pool of blood. It had been given the time to dry to flaking rust.

"I thought you said that on the other jobs here, nothing got on the carpet?" Holt hesitantly asked.

"Correct," said Ephraim. "I was here every time. I didn't miss anything like this, son. I can tell you that much."

Holt dropped to his haunches next to Ephraim, fascinated. "What can you, like, *read* from it, Elder?" he asked.

Ephraim snorted, then rose back to his feet with popping knees and a hand from the young man. "Nothing. Neither can anyone else, for that matter. Turns out that 'blood spatter analysis' is bullcrap. Pretty much all I can see is that there was a sizable pool here some point."

"But..." Holt felt like he was missing some vital component of a story problem. "Why is Mr. Stewart trying to hide this stain?"

"The guilt of blood," Ephraim answered, and then the lights went out.

Ephraim wouldn't have said he *screamed*, exactly, but he certainly yelped. With a pop that sounded like a blown fuse or an imploding lightbulb, all the lights in **COLD DEAD HANDS'** gun range died. The grimy overhead fluorescents, the work lights; all of them. The darkness unveiled by the light's abdication was absolute, thunderous, and pregnant with a sense of watchfulness.

"Oh hell," barked Ephraim, and this refocused Holt's attention. Bishop Ephraim Allred cursing on the job? He found it strangely reassuring. "Did you pack any battery lights, Holt?" Ephraim asked in a much calmer tone.

"Uh, let me check." Holt withdrew his phone, hit its LED flashlight, and picked his way to the equipment bags. The LED provided just enough brittle light to avoid obstacles and pitch great, wheeling bars of shadow across the gloomy walls.

"Looks like all we've got is handheld UV," Holt reported. He withdrew three long, bar-shaped lamps.

"That'll be fine," Ephraim assured him, accepting one as Holt returned. "I've just got to find the fuse box."

"Gotcha," Holt said. With a crisp click, both men turned on the UV hand lamps. For a moment, neither spoke.

"Elder, uh..." Holt began, but Ephraim silenced him with a clipped "*Quiet.*"

The otherworldly glow of the UV lamps provided only dim illumination. They cast the cavernous range in a muted luminescence but glared vividly from lighter surfaces. The floor around the men (the strip where the carpet had lain) was the palest patch, and offered up a vivid, mystifying glow. The glow, however, was only intermittent: broad swaths of the floor looked as though they'd been painted in splashes, spats, and swaths of jet black.

Ephraim knew what this photoreaction meant. Exposed to UV light, human blood absorbs the entirety of the spectrum. Bloodstains thus presented an appropriate appearance in their inky malignity. The quantity of blood and number of stains on display in the range was far too many for three humans to have left. *Or ten, for that matter*, Ephraim thought. The range had looked banal and dingy in the cheap fluorescent lights and unforgiving halogens. Now, it looked more like a killing floor.

"Stay here," Ephraim told Holt. He wound around the dead-eyed halogens and through the rental room. To his surprise, a mellow, caramel-colored glow of light emanated from the retail storefront. Sure enough, the showroom's arsenal was still lit by the indirect glow of the store's lights. *Well, heck*, thought Ephraim, *at least it's not the power. Just a fuse.* He was surprised to find Walter glowering and holding his phone aloft as though offering it in grumpy supplication to some unseen, angelic presence.

"What did Willy say?" Ephraim asked.

"I didn't get *ahold* of Willy," Walter snapped, waggling his phone.

"No signal?"

Walter's woolly eyebrows wove into a glower. "That's the weird part. Full bars. It must be some problem with Willy's phone. I don't get no ring, no voicemail, nothing."

Ephraim sighed and ran a hand over his silver, crewcut hair. "Well, we've got a situation that takes precedence." He glanced around at the lit displays. "No power outage in here? Did the lights flicker?"

Walter cocked an eyebrow in reply.

"Power's out on the range," Ephraim explained.

Now it was Walter's turn to sigh. "Any idea where the fuse box is?"

"Nope," said Ephraim. It was the darndest thing, he reflected. It wasn't just that the retail area of the shop was lit and the range wasn't. The glow of the buttery display lights coated the matte black and chrome silver weapons on display like holy oil but seemed to fall no farther than the threshold of the doorway. *Some trick of the shadows*, he thought.

"You'd better see this," he explained and led the way.

When Ephraim fanned his handheld lamp over the floor of the range, Walter emitted a pungent curse that caused the prim church elder to flush. Blood had been spilled *everywhere*. Walter and Ephraim were old hands in the business and knew what this unearthly galaxy of jet implied. The gore had been invisible by ordinary light, but blood *stains* show up under UV—even if they've been mopped up in an attempt to hide them.

"I'll bet you a box of donuts that when we get the lights back on and have a look we'll see scour marks," Walter mused. "This goes way past some bad news that the paper didn't report. This looks like gangland stuff." He shook his head. "I've known Willy Stewart for almost a decade. I don't care for him, but he doesn't seem capable of whatever I'm seeing."

"He doesn't seem smart enough," Ephraim agreed, drawing a grim smile from Walter.

"Hand me that lamp." Walter withdrew his phone, flicked on the LED flashlight, and handed it to Ephraim in exchange for a handheld UV light.

Ephraim swept the phone's flat gleam across the range and started as he saw Holt standing halfway down the concrete chute—midrange, as the gun fellows would say. The boy's back was turned to Ephraim. His shoulders were slumped, and his head cocked to one side. One arm jutted out at the elbow, his hand crooked in a strange, unnatural-looking claw. The sight was so jarring that Ephraim gasped and nearly dropped Walter's phone.

"Holt, good grief! What are you doing? Get back over here!" The bishop's heart hammered in his chest. Ephraim didn't like to see Holt standing there in the wide gullet of the range where so many bullets flew so often, irrational as that was. The young man seemed in harm's way somehow, standing there, as though he might slip back or forth in time by hours and wind up riddled by bullets. Ephraim hailed the boy again: "Hey! Holt!"

Holt stood very still and made no response.

"What the hell," Walter muttered, but his words weren't directed at Ephraim or Holt. Slowly, methodically, Walter moved the UV lamp back and forth across the patch of intermittently illuminated floor around him. He was attempting to calculate how many bodies must have bled out to leave such a scene. The number seemed improbably high. Whether **COLD DEAD HANDS** was concealing an epidemic of self-harm or some sick, after-hours snuff club, this was just too much death to have flown beneath the Salt Lake Valley's collective radar.

Ephraim extended one hand hesitantly toward his young protégé. When his fingers were still an inch from Holt's shoulder, Ephraim drew them back with a hiss of surprised pain. A cold rolled off the younger man, so fierce it burned like the surface of a lit stove. The freezing radiance should have fogged the air. It had no place in **COLD DEAD HANDS**, let alone near Holt's unprotected flesh.

The light in Walter's UV lamp imploded with a brittle, hollow *POCK!* Its gloomy luminescence winked out. Soundlessly, the flashlight on the phone in Ephraim's hand blinked off. For a moment, all was silent darkness.

Holt began to scream.

The shriek was deafening. At first, it hardly seemed human. Ephraim gave a shrill, surprised scream of his own. Walter lost his balance atop his hamstrings and toppled over. Holt's wail was an inarticulate, strangely toneless sound, as though it had been pressed from some ungodly bellows made of demoniacal meat and not a human throat. Just as Walter and Ephraim could bear no more, it petered out at the expiration of his breath and ended in a ragged sob.

A series of loud clicks and thrums coursed across the range as the fluorescents and halogens snapped on, died, and then were resurrected in syncopated strobes. This chaos made the scene around them seem nightmarishly more incomprehensible than mere darkness would have been. The shuttering, explosive light made the concrete room a bewildering wilderness of half-seen shapes. Shadows leaped and sprang with frightening rapidity. Support columns lent leaning bars of darkness to the fray.

Walter and Ephraim both saw what—or rather *who*—arrived with the storm of light. The dead had come to **COLD DEAD HANDS** in diverse, morbid forms. They glared with glittering black eyes, sunken in their parchment flesh. They gawped with mouths that drooled black blood and dislodged tongues. Torn jawbones loomed above aprons of wet gore and scattered, pearly teeth. They came with faces split by violence, pocked by self-annihilation, and contorted in un-comprehending pain.

They came and they weren't silent. *Atone*, they whispered, moaned, and sobbed. *ATONE* they shrieked. *Atone with blood*, the dead cajoled, *with blood. Spilled on the honest earth, that the smoke thereof might fly to heaven as an offering for your sins. Atone for the abuse, the crimes, the doubt or loneliness or debt. Come atone, Elder Ephraim Allred, for the fractures in your faith. Atone, scoffer Walter Specht, and scoff no more. Atone, Holt Hansen, for the many sins yet to come. Atone, and join the sea salt of your blood with this good ground, this black beach on the shore of death and—*

"DON'T LISTEN!" Walter roared. The spell was briefly broken. Ephraim lunged for Holt, and this time there was no unearthly cold, just his warm and solid shoulder. Ephraim gripped him fiercely and spun him around. Holt's eyes fluttered; a kid awakened in the middle of the night.

"What?" asked Holt in an absent tone. "*What?*"

Ephraim hauled Holt bodily off the gun range and to a stumbling crouch beside Walter. Walter, for his part, squeezed his eyes tightly closed and muttered passionately. Ephraim recognized the words as Latin. He knew that Walter had attended parochial school, but their few conversations on the subject had left him with no inkling that the old skeptic could still recall the Oratio Dominica (known to most as the Lord's Prayer).

The spectral light show engulfed the trio. One moment, there was darkness so absolute that it struck Ephraim as a foretaste of the wilderness beyond Heavenly Father's light. The next, annihilating radiance dawned like the star nearest the throne of God. *Atone*, the dead moaned all the while: *atone with blood and let its smoke ascend*. Terrified, Ephraim added his voice to Walter's. As he did, he wove his hands into the other man's white-knuckled grip. Ephraim didn't pray in Latin, of course. Ephraim prayed in Spanish; a prayer he remembered from a seldom-thought-of night half a century ago. On that night, he and his mission companion had cast something out of an old man bound to a bed in a slum in Lima.

Ephraim felt the warmth and strength of something surge into him, just as surely as he felt the presence of something cold and dark around them. It was a complicated feeling. What Ephraim felt surge within him wasn't God, precisely. The power seemed inchoate, mindless, more like magnetism than a mind. It felt like *Life*, in all its complicated, painful, and exuberant complexity. A breath of Life rose within Ephraim, Holt, and Walter. It flared like a clutched coal, small but fierce against the night.

The baleful presence in the room defied Ephraim's comfortable theology. It wasn't evil, but just as surely as the power clawing its way through Ephraim with painful ferocity was Life, this calm, cold, calculating, and eternal presence around them was Death. Death, which had accumulated like the gravity of a dying star until its pull drew vulnerable souls to **COLD DEAD HANDS**.

The current running through them vanished. The three men slumped in terror and exhaustion. In the fallout of the ghastly burst of light, the long fluorescent bulbs above them popped then hummed and slowly strobed to life. Ephraim was the first to recover his composure. He stood, placed his hands on his hips, and took in the scene around them. Without the UV lamp's otherworldly illumination, no evidence of anything abnormal was evident. He didn't for a moment doubt the reality of what had just occurred, but he *did* wonder if any trace of the visitation remained. Particularly any trace he could report to the police.

Ephraim helped Walter and Holt to their feet. In short order, the three performed an experiment at Ephraim's behest. They turned off the fluorescents and the halogens and, igniting the UV lamp, Walter swept it over the range once more. No trace of the bloodstains remained—other than the one they'd come to clean. Walter the empiricist did not care for this result.

"What in the hell," he sighed, "was all that blood about? If what we saw... Well, if..."

As Walter trailed off, Ephraim stepped in. "If it was real?" He shrugged. "Walter, we've known each other a long time. You've had some fun at my expense regarding my taste for local history, yes?" This drew a smile from Walter.

"The settlement of this valley wasn't quite as peaceful as most folks like to believe," Ephraim opined. "Executions. Suicide. Good, old-fashioned murder. If we could see the blood that's underneath the crust of modern life? I wonder if it wouldn't look like what we saw here tonight. I think at some point," he concluded, "this place became a black hole of blood."

They mulled that over. Holt spoke up first. "So, what now?"

Ephraim and Walter gave a pair of complementary shrugs.

"Now," Walter said, "we clean."

At 5 AM, Willy Stewart goosed his truck into the parking lot of **COLD DEAD HANDS**. His own hands were quite toasty, courtesy of his heated steering wheel. Talk radio blasted from his stereo loudly enough to proffer the proverbial red pill to any sheeple within a twenty-foot radius. He pulled around to the rear lot where, per their arrangement, Walter, Holt, and Ephraim waited. *The three of them seemed calm enough*, Willy noted, his beady eyes flicking over their faces for signs of supernatural distress. They seemed impatient but certainly not primed to rave and spread wild rumors. Willy had the pull to quash that sort of talk and a wallet padded well enough to employ new help whenever old help started acting twitchy. *And speaking of my wallet* Willy thought and killed his engine. He dropped to the concrete and rambled over to the **BIO KLEEN** crew.

"Mornin'!" Willy chirped.

None of them smiled or said a word. Willy's grin dried up, but at least one of the old buzzards detached himself from the trio to address him.

"All done," Ephraim said and tapped the card reader on his tablet as he passed it over. It was a brutally direct *pay me* gesture.

"I guess you must be in a hurry," Willy said, rankled at the **BIO KLEEN** man's lack of tact. He quashed his ire, keeping his discomfiture within the bounds of Utah passive aggression.

"All right," Willy said, extracting his credit card from his billfold. He made a show of reading the invoice line by line. He was glad he did. With a start, he glanced up at Ephraim.

"What the heck is *this*?" he demanded, tapping the screen.

This guy is Utah's biggest arms dealer, Ephraim thought, *and he can't bring himself to say, "What the hell?"*

"That," Ephraim replied, "is a surcharge. For extraordinary services."

"Yeah, well," frothed Willy, "the limit we set was $2,000. That says *twenty* thousand."

"We charge two thousand for extraordinary cleaning if the building is unoccupied while we work," explained Ephraim, never breaking eye contact with him. "If we have to deal with interruptions, it's an additional six thousand."

"What are you talking about?" Willy said in a resentful tone, but Walter saw his eyes flick down and to one side. "None of my employees were here last night."

"It doesn't matter who was here," responded Ephraim. "It's your responsibility to clear the building. And before you ask, young Holt back there was treated very *shabbily* in your establishment last night. The extra ten's for him—and you'll pay it so we keep our mouths shut." Willy's eyes betrayed something hard to pin down, something Ephraim thought he could interpret anyway.

"Are you *sure* none of your staff were here last night?" he asked gently.

Willy winced bodily, signed hastily, and handed him the tablet back. Ephraim had no way of knowing about Willy's twentysomething nephew Levi, a longtime store adoptee who had worked and shot there since his teens. He'd stayed late one night four years ago to "help with inventory." That night, in the darkness, Levi died by his own hand on the gun range. That time, Ephraim had done the cleaning up himself.

"Thank you for your business, Mr. Stewart," Ephraim said. "If you have needs in the future, please don't call us. Under any circumstances." He turned back to his crew.

"Hang on—just *hang on*!" Willy cried. "The surcharge is fine! Honest!"

Ephraim stopped. He slowly turned back. "How many?" he demanded. "How *many* trauma cleaning companies worked jobs on that range and quit before you called us?"

Willy's downturned mouth and cagey-looking eyes were all the answer Ephraim needed.

As the cleaning crew clambered into their van, Willy Stewart watched them go. He thought about his shop. Thought about the long nights closing up, sometimes by himself. Of whispers he couldn't explain, and power outages that defied diagnosis. He thought about blood debt, and of atonement, and the smoke of sacrifice.

He turned, regarded **COLD DEAD HANDS'** shadowy storefront, and meditated on his little patch of thirsty earth.

"Past Future Imperfectly Tense"

Michelle Hartman

A quiet motel room, Highway 40
far enough from wives in Vernal.
Night air slides across windowsill,
whisper dries erotic sweat.
Errant lovers are sleeping
come closer, close enough to smell
gin, perspiration, and perfume.

Near enough to trace
curves, hips, and biceps.

The dead are watching too.
They slip though termite-carved
wall cavities, worn linoleum
and dust-dulled carpets.

Foot of bed leans a shadowy stonemason,
his vacant mind still ringing
with chime of chisel strike.

A smoky lady hovers by bedhead,
she walks this night stop haunting
an escaped lover,
as quiet in death as in life.

Long-departed truckers scratch and stretch.
Salesmen drift by pondering
new sales pitch.
Conmen and Hookers collect at the door
still expectant about future.

The adulterous sleep; the dead gather
towards midnight, farmers, sailors,
thieves, and Saints,
Government clerks and lawyers join the vigil.

Rowdy children run mouths open
with giggles no longer heard.
Babies crawl crying through an unformed forever.

Don't move, the dead draw
near, wring their hands, in sorrow or glee.

Wait for the bedmates to open
their eyes so they can be seen.
They only want to be seen.

"I'M NOT YOUR MOTHERFUCKING SUNSHINE"

Bryan Stubbles

You hate the song "You Are My Sunshine." Absolutely loathe it. You despise it worse than you despise your workplace, a restaurant called Hardtack Box. But here you are. A Grade Zero schlub dude doing schlub work at America's finest schlub restaurant. The workers secretly call it the "Heart Attack Box." It's December 1997 in Layton, Utah, a suburban nightmare of cookie-cutter homes arrayed in off-white, white, beige, and off-beige. It's midnight, but the snow outside brightens everything like an incandescent light. May as well be daytime. Your scheduled shift lasts all night, ten p.m. to six a.m.

Cleaning the grease traps on the grill line? Piece of cake. Sweeping the floors? Like shooting fish in a barrel.

Hardtack Box is the type of restaurant that would happen if Colonel Harlan Sanders opened a restaurant with former Alabama governor George Wallace.

The restaurant is packed with more faux nostalgia than a fake 50s diner. A literal school desk nailed to the wall? Check. A pile of vintage books held together by a leather strap on the wall? Check. Snowshoes hanging on the wall? Check. Old radio episodes of *Amos 'n' Andy* in the gift shop? Better believe it. *Fibber McGee and Molly*? Of course.

The usual piped-in shitty country music has been replaced by piped-in shitty Christmas music. "Good King Wenceslas" can get fucked. Same deal with Dasher, Dancer, Comet, and Stupid. If only The Little Drummer Boy played a bongo. Then it might be interesting.

Weird stuff happens in the middle of the night in weird restaurants. There was the time you and a trainee were the only souls in the building. You both heard the front door open and assumed it was the manager. Except when you checked, the front door was still locked and chained. There was that time you saw a blur knock over a garbage can. You're still not sure what that was.

Then there is "You Are My Sunshine." Amongst the kitschy knick-knacks and campy bric-à-brac, a plastic and metal sunflower keeps vigil in front of a window in the gift shop. A singing plastic sunflower. A motion-activated singing sunflower. A one-hit wonder that cranks out "You Are My Sunshine" every time someone walks past it. The voice used in this song of doom is a cross between a young Brenda Lee and Steve Urkel.

Not only does it sing, but its leaves twist, its stem wriggles, and hidden eyes and a mouth open to lip sync that shitty song. You despise the hellish sunflower.

Naturally, the sunflower has a multitude of boxed-up sunflowers underneath it, ready to sell at a moment's notice. For only $15.95 plus tax, any customer can bring home the shittiness that is Hardtack Box.

Once, you turned it off and your rotund fake-smiley manager lost his shit over it and threatened to give your shift to another worker. He forbade you to turn the sunflower off. You do your best not to walk near it and trigger it. That usually works. No motion, no song.

You've now been alone for a couple of hours. You're aggressively mopping the dining area floor. There's still silverware here and there along with discarded napkins. Not only do Hardtack Box's patrons have bad taste, but it feels like they purposefully make your life more difficult.

"Carol of the Bells," one of the better Christmas songs, comes on. Beneath the music, you faintly hear something: that friggin' "Sunshine" song. You sigh. You go from the dining area through a too big walkway into the gift shop area. You can hear the song playing. Once you're inside the gift shop, it mysteriously stops.

"What the fuck?" you ask yourself. You walk back to the dining area to continue the drudge work.

After mopping the dining area, your work takes you to the kitchen and "the line," where all the food is prepared. True to its name, it's a narrow path through a collection of grills. You get to scrub the congealed grease off the floor. Lucky you. This part of the restaurant is music-free during your shift. *Gott sei Dank*. It's music-free until you hear that ominous "Sunshine" creep in like an unwanted uncle. You lean your giant mop-sized scrub brush against the grill. You walk through the kitchen and the dining room until you again reach the gift shop. Of course, the music stops. This time, you turn the sunflower off. Fuck your asshole manager. As you turn it off, you hear something fall in the kitchen.

"Fuck you," you tell the sunflower. You get back to work. The giant scrubber is knocked over. That's what you'd heard.

Bland tedium follows. You scrub the grease off the floor. Most of it anyways. You think of people who are asleep now. They'll wake up to a fresh blanket of snow.

The cool thing about not having a boss on site while you work is you can work as fast or slow as you like. Tonight, would be a "hurry and get it done" night. You savor your free time.

You finish washing down the grills from the line. A couple of hours of blissful nothingness await you. You go to the sparse breakroom. The only objects of interest there are a two-day-old *Salt Lake Tribune* and a Spanish-English dictionary.

According to the newspaper, five people died in weekend car accidents. You check the basketball scores. The Jazz beat Orlando, 98-93. Just a few days before, the Jazz had stomped the Magic by over thirty points. You fold the newspaper into a little Napoleon hat. Just as you press the final crease, that same "Sunshine" song starts up again. You stand up and carry the paper hat to the gift shop.

The sunflower is playing the song. The positioning has changed. Its deceptively plaintive face stares at you as if seeking approval. You're not here to dish out approval. You turn the sunflower over, open up the small latch underneath, and remove the four AA batteries.

"Try singing without batteries, motherfucker," you tell the sunflower.

You put the sunflower back on its perch and place the newspaper hat on it, making sure to pull the paper down far enough to cover as much of the sunflower's face as possible. Definitely an improvement.

The gift shop echoes with the powerful vocals of Mariah Carey saying she wants you for Christmas. She couldn't handle you. You walk back to the breakroom.

You flip through the Spanish-English dictionary. "Ábaco" means abacus. "Bidón" means a large can or drum. "Dedo corazón" is the middle finger. In English we could call it the "dick finger," not the "heart finger." Speaking of dick fingers, you hear a commotion in the gift shop. You investigate.

Back in the gift shop, the newspaper hat lies shredded on the floor. The sunflower sits high above it. You look at it. It starts to sing that dreaded song. The problem is, you're about twenty feet away. The sunflower also lacks batteries. Those are back in the breakroom. The volume of the singing sunflower increases by the second.

"I'm not your motherfucking sunshine!" you yell at the serenading flower. It pays no heed and continues singing like the piece of metal, plastic, and sick Americana it is.

You look around. You pick up a snow globe. You throw it at the sunflower, scoring a direct hit that sends the sunflower to the floor. The mechanical motions make it look like it's writhing as it warbles.

"What the fuck is wrong with you?" you ask. Eartha Kitt's "Santa Baby" comes on. Finally, something good on the Christmas loop.

You check the clock. Four a.m. Time to start the food prep. Even though you're the night maintenance worker, you have to bake biscuits and cook gravy. The gravy is disgustingly vile. The restaurant stores the concentrated gravy in tubes in the giant walk-in freezer. Your job is to cut open the plastic tubes, dump them in a giant pot, and add buttermilk.

The giant pots contain a lever for easy dumping.

You walk to the freezer and grab the massive tube of gravy concentrate. You hear something moving along the floor in the kitchen. You look outside the freezer. That sunflower is sidewinding along the floor. You throw the tube of gravy at it. You miss. This is why you were never a quarterback. The song plays again as the flower inches toward you.

"This is stupid," you say to yourself.

You grab the tube off the floor. You approach the flower. You batter it with the tube of gravy.

"Fuck you! Fuck you! Fuck you! Fuck you! Fuck you!"

The damn thing is now all busted up. Its leaves writhe on the floor. The jaw bit is also broken loose. One eye doesn't open. You fucked that sunflower up. Then, the song starts again. This time you step on it. Hard. You're not finished. You take a long knife from the grill line and stab the sunflower in its stupid sunflower face. Your knife goes through the sunflower. The sunflower finally stops singing.

You rip open the frozen gravy tube and dump it into one of the industrial-sized pots. You grab a gallon of buttermilk and dump it in and turn the pot to "high." It should take a while to fully melt and gravy-ize.

"Dumb fucking sunflower," you say. Then a sound hits you: a chorus of "You Are My Sunshine." You turn. A legion of singing sunflowers surrounds you. It must be the restaurant's entire stock. You kick some out of the way. Others take their place.

"This is ridiculous," you say to no one in particular. You try to step over them until one jumps up and hammers you in the balls. Not a glancing blow, but an incapacitating hit that sends you to the floor. Now the sunflowers have leveled the playing field. They swarm you.

Those movable leaves? They dig into your flesh and churn out something akin to hamburger. That twisty stem? One broken-off twisty stem twists its way into your innards. The knife you impaled the poor little sunflower with? It's in your fucking eye.

Everything turns red. The sunflowers do not let up. You'll pay dearly. A couple dozen sunflowers cut you down like Caesar in Rome.

You smell something. Gravy. Fuck. That's right. The pot is nearby. It has a massive handle. You wipe the blood out of your good eye only to see two smiling, singing sunflowers atop the pot. They smile right at you before pulling the lever to make the gravy flow.

You scream as you feel the gooey liquid scald your skin and burn your wounds. At least you think you scream. You can't hear anything over the deafening din of "You Are My Sunshine."

"Shadow Over Salt Lake"

Johnny Worthen

L ucy had been trying to get me to meet the old man for weeks. She'd run into him at a girl's night out with her friends. They'd rolled into this bar, she said, three daiquiris to the good, and then, half on a dare, approached the anachronistic old timer in the corner. Flirting turned to conversation turned to rapt attention as he told them a tale that sobered them up quick and sent Lucy home to me, shaken, demanding I meet this guy.

Four Fridays later, four trips to this dive bar on the west side, there he sat, a grizzled old man. His face was creviced by sun and wind, more eroded than aged. His beard was just white wisps touching his chin over a comb mustache that covered his mouth entirely. The ends of that were gnawed off. When he looked up at us approaching, I saw pale eyes beneath drooping lids, pre-cataract if not full-on blind. He was nursing a watery drink because this being Utah, that's all they serve.

"Do you remember me?" asked Lucy, leaning over the table. He didn't seem to recognize her, looked at her as if seeing her anew, more than likely not seeing her at all with those milky eyes.

"You told us a story about the Great Salt Lake a couple weeks back. Do you remember?"

"I told ya' that story?" he said, or maybe croaked.

"You did. Would you mind telling it again? For my husband. Say hi, Jack."

I said hi, feeling like a total jackass, still not sure why Lucy wouldn't tell me the story herself, and instead turned probably a ten-minute conversation into a four-week quest, her on edge every minute of it.

"I don't often tell that story, but I been telling it more lately," said the man. "Cause the water is getting where it need be for the trouble."

Lucy gave me an excited look and took a chair at the table. The man finished his drink watching us sit. I pulled a chair out for myself and, before I'd settled, a waitress came with another drink for the man, and we ordered a round. He was drinking rye whiskey and water—I didn't think they still made rye. Lucy ordered a Manhattan; I had a local IPA. The waitress asked if I wanted a glass. I did. Maybe it was a dig. I'm not sure. It was Lucy who understood bar culture, not me. I tend to stay in, go to my friends' houses, or have them over for cards and beers. Just different settings. Less clean-up Lucy's way. I'm not the jealous type, but luckily, Lucy's never given me cause to prove it.

"You paying for this, young man?" asked the old-timer.

"Of course, he is," said Lucy.

"Sure," I said. "Cheers."

"Bad luck to cheers without a glass. We'll wait for yours to come."

We did. We sat and waited, saying nothing in the noisy bar until the waitress came back. I glanced at Lucy, wondering what was happening, but she just nodded. I guess this was how the spell worked.

We got our drinks and raised a glass to toast each other. I'd pulled a deep draught before I realized I was drinking out of the bottle. I poured the rest of the foam into my chilled glass and felt the waitress shaking her head behind me somewhere.

"In the cowboy days, Indians didn't live near the lake," he began. I opened my mouth to correct him, to use the politically correct term, but a kick from Lucy shut me up. "They hardly came into the valley at all. When the pligs came in—" My eyes rolled, but I avoided a kick this time and just weathered Lucy's sidelong 'shut up and let the man talk' look. "They said 'this was the place' cause there weren't no one else here. There was a reason for that."

He paused.

I scanned the bar for other racists, expecting to see a Gadsden flag or the stars and bars. Nope. Not even an antler. Just trendy neon lights illuminating hipsters drinking IPAs out of bottles. The air smelled of chemical fruits exhausted from ubiquitous vape pens.

The quiet stretched on. I said, "Okay, I'll bite. Why didn't any native peoples live near the lake?"

"Who?"

Lucy gave me no input. "The uhm... Indians," I said as quietly as I could. "Why didn't they—anyone—live in the valley? Was it because of the salt or something?"

"Them."

"Them?"

"You a reader, son?" the man asked me.

"Me? Yeah, I'd say so."

"You ever read about Innsmouth?"

I racked my brain. The name was familiar, but I couldn't put my finger on it.

"'Them' was mentioned in that story. Others too," he said. "If you knew those stories, it'd make things easier. But don't matter."

I watched the foam settle in my glass, trying to feel for Lucy, who had seemed so shocked after meeting this man. I couldn't see it, but something happened that night to turn a middle-aged dietitian into a scared rabbit.

"The legends, near as I heard from someone who heard from someone who heard from an Indian—a Ute, a local man—is that they stopped feeding them. When they fed them, things were fine, or at least they left folks alone. But then the Utes didn't have the people to spare. So, they stopped feeding them and then they had to get the hell out of this valley. Ran to the desert. To the high, dry desert."

"People?"

"That's right. They fed them people. Nothing else would do."

"You gotta back up old-timer, what are we talking about?"

"I don't know a white man can pronounce it right. Doubt the Indians did either. Imagine a fish choking up a piece of chum and you come close."

"A fish choking up chum?" I said.

"Cho-gak," rasped the old man. "Cho-gaskh. Something like that."

"That's 'them?'"

He sipped his drink. "Yeah. They're in the lake. They're in all water of any notice. Usually, they're sleeping. Dormant. Maybe tucked up in eggs, buried in the hardening mud, or something. Waiting. But sometimes, they're awake."

"They don't actually eat the people," said Lucy to me. "Tell him," to the man.

"They eat plenty of them, but not all. No. Not all. See, there's a deal that's made. An arrangement. An old contract between men and those slimy beasts."

"Slimy?"

"Slimy. Not an insult but an observation of what was seen. Slimy people. Fish people. Unblinking eyes, scales. Fins. Men once. Now... Shogawk."

I wanted to point out that he'd changed the name of 'them' again but left it alone.

"I once found a smart guy, a scientist, who knew about amphibians. They're the weirdest thing. Land and water. They're sensitive to climate change. First to notice when the water's poisoned. They die or maybe they change—grow new legs, third eyes. Adapt and survive. Quick to evolve. They're tough. They're old. Very old. Before us. Long before us. Maybe the rightful owners of this planet. Who knows?"

Okay, I thought. Maybe this old guy did belong in this bar where giving the earth back to slugs made political sense.

"I've heard that in some places, they made a good bargain with the people. Gold and fish in that one story. Utes got the short stick. Their gift was to be left alone. Ain't much to recommend throwing your young people into the lake if all you get is that nothing changes. But once they didn't, well, they came out and took what they wanted."

"People?"

"Yeah, people. Some they ate, and some they changed to be like them. Them that can walk out easier than the others. I suspect most of them can't, the pure breed. The people ones—the ones that were folk—they became the ones who easily come out and get the others. So, it was the Indians' own people who dragged their others into the lake those times."

"You seem to know a lot about these Shogaths," I said.

"Just what I figured from the stories, speculation based on the stories, feelings, and what I seen on the shores." His gaze fell far away and his eyes murkier, if that was possible. "But it tracks."

"Tell us why you're telling everyone about this now," said Lucy egging him on.

"Yeah, don't stop the spooky tale now," I said.

He looked at me and nodded knowingly. "'Course you don't believe it. Who'd believe a person that looked like me? I'm a homeless coot, right? Out of my mind? Maybe a Western cosplayer from a comic convention. Don't matter. I tell you the story, because your lady here wants me to, and because time's running out. Folk need to know the story so we can prepare. Not to stop them—I doubt anyone will believe the stories enough to prevent anything—but when it happens, if the idea is there already, in our heads, then maybe our minds won't snap when we see them. That's a common detail in all the stories. Folks freeze when they see them, shut down for the horror. It makes them easy vittles. Just glancing at these things is enough to break a man's mind if he lacks the imagination to pre-suspect such things." He seemed to grow bigger and straighter. He raised his hand, and I thought of a preacher on a pulpit. "Anyone who harbors hope of redemption, or some faith in righteousness, or any superiority is done for. The world ain't ours. Ain't full of goodness. It's theirs. They're just letting us live in it for now."

The waitress brought us fresh drinks. The man shrank back to his usual size as his empty glass was replaced with a full one. He nodded to me in thanks for the new one, so I guess I was on the hook for another round. Another beer for me. Lucy's glass was barely touched.

"The water level of the lake has changed so much in these last years that they're stirring. Water pulled away to bake the mud to cement and then all rushed back this season, wetting them again. Now they're hatching."

"Get real," I said.

"Ever wonder why there ain't no buildings out that way? You watch real estate? Every square mile of this valley is being developed. Not around the lake. Know why? Because there's a law that says you can't. Them pligs heard the story, and God bless them, they believed enough of it to take a few precautions. They bought us a little space."

"The airport is out that way."

"Not on the lake."

I knew that no one built near the lake because of the smell and the flies and the fact that the land was for shit. I also doubted that there was any kind of nineteenth-century ordinance that forbade development near it. Hadn't they just built a new prison out that way? But he was on a tear now. Why slow down his story with a few facts?

"They're hatching. In darkness, they slither out, young ones and old ones. They seek the deep water and meet their kind. There they wait. Regather. Maybe nothing will come of it this time. Maybe not enough water change. Maybe it ain't the sign they were waiting for, but it might be."

"Why kind of sign?"

"The end of the world. The waking of the Old Ones."

"Cthulhu?" I said. "Oh my God, you're repurposing Lovecraft stories! Oh, come on..."

"Truth hidden in fiction," he said. "But don't matter. They're hatching. I seen them. I smelled them. I heard them rise from the sucking black muck and slither their slimy bodies into the water. They gotta be hungry. They're a lot of them."

"Think about it," said Lucy. "Global warming. Isn't that the end of the world? The water rising? It fits."

"Oh, for crying out loud," I said.

The man sipped his drink. Lucy looked earnestly concerned.

The lights blinked.

"What the...?" said Lucy.

"What? Our electrical grid can't handle summer air conditioners. Infrastructure is for shit. Nothing new."

They blinked again and then went out. Emergency lights came on, blinding spots in the corners casting harsh beams into the bar, lighted signs showing the exits. The bar fell silent and then erupted in a rush—cell phone messages, lights, and squeals.

This is an emergency alert. Stay tuned for important information.

"Let's get out of here," said Lucy and took my hand.

I dropped a twenty on the table for the drinks and then dug out another ten. Probably still not enough. The man watched me.

"Get to high ground," he said. "Dry land as soon as you can."

"That'll help?" I said.

"Probably not."

We followed a slow exit onto the street. The city was dark save for cars and a few lights in the bank, obviously running on generators.

The wind was from the northwest. If you know the city, you know what that means. The fishy stench of the Great Salt Lake carried on cold air. It wafted in around us like a shroud. It was the strongest I'd ever smelled it—rotting shrimp, dying weeds, dead gulls.

Lucy gripped my arm like I was her lifeline.

"Do you hear that?"

I listened.

On the reeking air came the distant sounds of shouts. Of screams. Of screams and screams. Then gunshots—a flurry of them, distant and brief. More screams.

"It's coming closer," she said.

"From which direction?"

"From the direction of the lake, of course."

"Oh, come on Lucy. Looters probably."

"Looters?"

"Yeah. People suck."

She looked at me like I'd failed to understand that one plus one equaled two. I knew, of course, what she was thinking; we were primed to imagine horror, but I wasn't going to fall for it.

"Let's get out of here." She pulled me on toward the car and tripped, breaking a heel. She ripped off her shoes and threw them away.

"Can't you fix that?"

"Shut up and get in the car."

"We're not going anywhere," I said pointing up the road. "The lights are out. It's gridlock. No cars moving anywhere. See? Might as well find a place to hole up. We should have stayed in the bar."

"No. It was in a basement."

"And that—"

A shape drew my attention down an alley, and I caught sight of something silhouetted by slow-moving headlights on the next block. It was the size of a man hunched over. It moved toward us. Not at a walk, more of a shamble. The headlights went past. I waited for a scream—expecting it, I hate to say, but it did not come. My eyes adjusted. There were a few lights that darted into the alley—star shine, a passing bike, a candle-lit window three stories up—and in those lights, the shape showed itself in flickering reflections as if he were silver or wet. Or slimy.

Headlights behind and the shape was again an outline. Closer, still shambling, and not alone. More shapes were moving behind it, coming alongside and then passing it. These shapes not walking, not even shambling. They were hopping.

The smell was thick, a sticking miasma of swamp mud.

I froze. My mind reeled in the horror of my imagination.

"They see us," said Lucy.

I could only stare, transfixed. Lucy obviously had more defense against this; perhaps what the man had said about being prepared mattered. She'd had a month to dwell on what I incredulously saw now; I'd only had a few minutes. But was I seeing it? Was I partially armored, or was I infected with imaginings that made me think I saw such things?

"Jack!"

I snapped back. "What?" I said.

She grabbed my arm, again too tightly, and pulled me along like I was a misbehaving toddler.

I followed her as she ran across the parking lot through the far alley and then up the street.

"Where are we going?" I asked.

"Susan's," she said. "High ground."

"Good a plan as any."

Around the next corner, we held up, sliding to a stop.

A car wreck. Three sedans piled up and on fire. Flames. Shadows. Screams and... and... and something else. Something guttural, gurgling. Wet.

I looked at Lucy. She jumped and her hand flew to her mouth, and I followed her gaze.

The light. It had to be the light. The priming in the bar and the light. The panic. The dark. The shadows.

What I saw was this. What I thought I saw was this. This... There were two mounds of slime with legs and arms, but slime, nonetheless, pulling at the body of a moaning man. One held him by a leg, the other an arm. They stretched him. The body split at the shoulder with a pop and a pink mist. Sloshing. We heard screams, not from him, but from up the street. Others were witnessing this too.

The one with the arm raised it to its head and opened its frog-like mouth, then drove the arm, wristwatch and all, down its gullet. It stood there placid for a moment and then parted its lips enough to allow a pustulent pink tongue to slither out and wipe its bulbous eyes like a squeegee before retracting back into the maw. The other creature knelt over the ripped and squirming man and gnawed on his knee.

"Help me!" the man shouted to someone we couldn't see. "Marci, help me!"

We didn't wait to see if Marci would help him. God forgive me, forgive us, we didn't help him either.

We turned and ran down another alley and across another street, shapes and screams all around us.

Susan's apartment building was four blocks on and, luckily, east.

We crossed a car-jammed street, then another. In the headlights, I saw the bottom of Lucy's feet, scratched, scoured, and bloody. My thought should have been to help her, to wrap her feet in my shirt or something, but what came to my mind was to ditch her because she was leaving a trail of blood those monsters could follow.

The next street, then the next, and we pulled up again. Another jam. A dozen cars hopelessly snarled together. We had to climb over hoods to get by. Honking and then screams.

We turned to look. I wish we hadn't. People were being ripped out of their cars. They didn't fight, just watched as the creatures opened their doors like they were hellish valets. Only when the slimy claws grabbed them did they scream. The horrors ignored the noise and patiently bit through the seat belts like so much sewing thread. We watched as they—different shapes of frog-fish-men—systematically moved from one car to the next, grabbing the frozen inhabitants and pulling them out.

Then a new horror.

A different thing. Smaller, squatter. More fishlike than frog. Tentacled. A writhing mound. A slithering tentacled mound, dotted with black unblinking eyes, high as a man's waist, wide as a dinner table, arms slapping for yards around it.

The frog men carried or tossed or regurgitated the people they'd captured onto the mound which caught them in its squishy side and then wrapped them in its wriggling arms. Then, when they were still, another appendage, this one with a spade-shaped top, slapped across their faces, covered their noses, and silenced their screaming mouths, leaving only their open, terrified, and searching eyes for us to see. In an instant, they fell limp and the mound dropped. The bodies slid down the scaly side to be still on the street. The mound then moved on to the next person. The used ones were collected and dragged westward.

We fled south, crossed another street, and then we were at Susan's building. The lights were out in it; the door locked, the intercom useless.

Lucy hopped on one foot, a bloody footprint beneath her. I bent down, finally, to give her my shoes.

"No," she said. "Kick in the door. I'll be alright."

The door wouldn't budge, but a window around the side gave way to a garbage can. I pushed the glass away, took off my shirt to cover what was left, and helped Lucy climb inside.

As I bent to follow her, I almost choked on the smell of muck, organic and thick, black and penetrating. It came in rush, a part of something behind me.

I didn't turn around. My mind was reeling. I was in a nightmare. That is what I knew. The rule of nightmares was to flee. I didn't turn around. I climbed in, and as I fell forward, the slosh of a slippery hand pulled off my shoe and that was enough to make me scream.

"John!"

I rushed toward the voice in the darkness. Lucy in a doorway, her phone used for light, the red emergency alert still glowing crimson red. No new updates.

We ran for the stairs and climbed the six floors to Susan's apartment in a heartbeat, every step we expected to hear the sloppy pursuit of the Shogaths. At the door, we pounded and pounded and pounded for entry. Susan didn't answer.

"She isn't home," said a man from next door. "What's—"

We rushed through his door and pulled the man inside with us as an afterthought. We locked his door and waited.

Some of our fear must have seeped out because the man silently accepted our presence, and stayed with us in the farthest bedroom, armed with golf clubs and paper weights.

And there we stayed through the night, til dawn. Til ten, til noon, til two o'clock, when the phones rang all clear and the power returned. Til four when we finally left our host and found our car right where we'd left it.

The streets were clean, though the smell lingered, the earthy salty fishy smell.

At home, we drank and slept behind double-locked doors. We stayed in for days.

The news detailed looting and mayhem in a load-related blackout. Deaths had been reported. Later in the week, in small articles buried deep in the secondary pages of the media web, were long lists of missing people from that night. Hundreds of missing people. Susan was among them. A few days after that came the mention of new planning regulations around the Great Salt Lake, condemnations, and permit refusals. Threats of lawsuits from a dozen builders. Then, breaking all precedent, it was announced that the governor had moved his official residence out of Salt Lake City to far away Kanab, deep in the high, dry desert.

"Moving Shadows"

Daniel Gene Barlekamp

The rusted wheels groaned to life. The side rods struggled into motion like the spindly arms of a mummy waking for the first time in four thousand years. The locomotive's whistle shrieked as it ejected a plume of black steam into the cloudless blue sky. Less than two minutes later, the train rumbled down the track, several tons of steel picking up speed with nowhere to go but forward.

I sat in the caboose with the others and watched the historic Canyon City Railroad Station vanish among the buttes. An ocean of brush extended as far as I could see in every direction, sitting dry and lifeless under the beating sun. If eastern Utah is one thing, it's hot. The mercury thermometer in the caboose already read 105 degrees Fahrenheit, and it was only going to get hotter from there.

This was going to be a long day and an even longer night.

The summer I turned eleven, my dad sent me to sleepaway camp for the first time just outside Moab. He wanted me to work on my social skills and forge lasting friendships, or something like that. I was supposed to go for a week, but I didn't last half that long. Each night, I lay awake as a pair of invisible hands wrapped themselves around my throat, finally waking my tentmates with my screams. After two nights, the counselors called my dad to pick me up, recommending that I get tested for generalized anxiety disorder. A year later, here I was on an overnight trip on an antique locomotive. My dad thought it was a good compromise: one afternoon and evening away, then back home the next day. Twenty-four hours spent speeding across the desert in a hot metal box.

What could go wrong?

"I wish there was air conditioning," Eliot said, removing his thick glasses to mop his brow with the hem of his bright-red Canyon City Railroad t-shirt. When he pulled his shirt back down, the smiling cartoon steam engine was dark with sweat.

"Uh, it's an antique train," Zack pointed out, snapping his gum. "Like, *vintage.*"

"Maybe if you keep complaining it'll cool off," Ruth added.

I could already feel the anxiety creeping up from where it always started: at the base of my neck, tickling me like dozens of tiny fingers. The heat and the bickering weren't helping, so I stood up.

"Where are you going?" Ruth asked.

"To explore the rest of the train," I said.

I was about to step from the caboose to the next car when a hand grabbed my arm. It was Eliot. He was smaller than the rest of us, and he looked up at me from behind his glasses.

"I'll come with you," he said.

"Have a nice date!" Zack called after us as we left.

We passed through a couple of mismatched boxcars from different decades before reaching the main attraction, where we were meant to spend most of our time: a Pullman passenger car from 1894. By craning our necks and peering down the side of the car, we saw that it was painted a grim gun-metal gray with P-U-L-L-M-A-N stenciled in Old West-style lettering beneath the windows. I stepped across the couplers connecting the cars and reached for the door handle.

Inside the Pullman, the shades were drawn, and we couldn't see the other end of the narrow corridor that stretched before us. On our right, a clunky radio transmitter sat on a metal table, demonstrating how the crew members communicated with each other from opposite ends of the train. A piece of plastic bread and a tin coffee cup made it appear that an engineer had just stepped away, even though no one had operated the radio for more than a century. In the dusky light, I read a plaque on the wall explaining that, back in the 1800s, traveling in a Pullman sleeper car like this one was considered the pinnacle of luxury.

I had taken only a couple of steps down the corridor before Eliot screamed behind me. When I turned around, he was standing with his back pressed flat against the wall, staring into one of the rooms.

"What is it?" I asked.

All he did was point.

I approached the open door and looked inside.

It was one of the bedrooms, with two bunks stacked one on top of the other, a small sink, and a mirror. In one of the corners, half hidden in the shadows, stood a woman. She wore a dress from the 1890s, drab olive green with gold trim, its hem brushing the floor, the shoulders stiff and padded. Her gloved hands extended straight out as though reaching for whoever passed by her door. Her face was stark white, with no features at all: no eyes, no nose, no mouth. She stood as still as a statue.

I quickly realized she *was* a statue—a mannequin dressed in 1890s fashion to complete the train's historical effect.

"For God's sake, Eliot, it's just a dummy," I said, letting out my breath. "Come on, keep up."

There were mannequins in all the rooms: three more women in dresses in the ladies' washroom, their hands poised above their wigs as if fixing their hair; a man in a three-piece suit sitting at a table in the dining parlor in front of a tray of artificial cakes; a boy alone in one of the bedrooms, facing the corner as though he had been sent into time-out. The car was nearly silent, the only sound coming from the roar of the wheels beneath the floor. Around us, the air felt dead, like the mannequins had sucked the life out of it with their blank faces and fake food.

At last, we reached the far end of the car.

"Let's go meet the engineer," I said as we pushed through the door.

After the oppressive darkness of the Pullman car, even the blinding desert sun felt inviting as it sank toward the horizon. Ahead was the locomotive's platform, protected on three sides by thin guardrails. The engineer sat with his back to us and concentrated on operating the engine, a snaking mass of iron pipes and valves.

"We'd better not bother him," I shouted into Eliot's ear over the hiss of the steam. "It'll probably be dinnertime soon, anyway."

We hurried back through the Pullman. On our way past the last bedroom, I could have sworn the boy mannequin was now facing the corridor, but I shook the idea from my head. So far, I had managed to keep the tingling fingers at bay, and I wanted them to stay there.

The rest of the late afternoon and early evening passed quickly. When it started to get dark, Eliot, Ruth, Zack, and I gathered in the Pullman car, where the crew—who we had yet to meet—had lit the rooms and corridors with imitation oil lamps. We ate in the dining room, surrounded by mannequins enjoying their meals in the surrounding booths. Afterward, we played round after round of Crazy Eights, War, and Memory until a booming voice announced over the intercom:

"Passengers, lights out will occur in ten minutes. Please find your way to your quarters."

Eliot and I shared a room. I let Eliot take the top bunk so he could stay as far as possible from the mannequin in our room. I thought about dragging it out to the corridor and shutting the door, but to be honest, I didn't want to go near enough to touch it. As the mysterious voice had warned, ten minutes later all the electric lamps were extinguished at once, plunging the Pullman into darkness. Eliot's breathing soon slowed and deepened in the upper bunk. I fell asleep watching the bright desert stars through our tiny window while trying to ignore the silhouette of the mannequin lurking in the corner of my eye.

I awoke a couple of hours later to a bloodcurdling shriek from a few rooms away. It sounded like Zack. I leaped out of bed and started for the door, then I froze.

Had the mannequin moved? I thought she had been facing the door, but now she was turned toward our bunks as if she were watching over them. Invisible fingers tickled the base of my neck.

"What is it?" Eliot asked.

"N-nothing," I stuttered. "Let's go see what happened."

The hallway was dark, lit only by the moonlight falling through the gaps in the shades. I flicked the switches on a couple of the lamps, but nothing happened.

We found Ruth standing in her pajamas outside the door to Zack's room.

"Where is he?" she asked, looking frantic.

"What do you mean?" I asked.

"Zack," she said. "He's just... gone."

From the other end of the Pullman, the side nearest the engine, came the sound of shattering glass, like one of the lamps had been swept off a table. Ruth started to jog in the direction of the sound.

"Where are you going?" I called after her.

"That might've been Zack," she shouted back as she vanished down the hallway.

Eliot tugged on my sleeve.

"We don't have to go, do we?" he asked.

"I... I don't know," I stammered. "We should probably stick together."

"But it's dark down there," he said.

"It's dark everywhere," I pointed out.

I took the first steps in the direction Ruth had gone, stepping over the fragments of a shattered plate in the dining car. Eliot didn't argue. He took my hand, and I let him. The air felt close and thick, and the corridor was silent except for the continuous thunder of the wheels. Each room we passed—bedrooms, washrooms, kitchen—was empty. No Zack, no Ruth... and no mannequins.

"Where is everyone?" Eliot asked once we reached the far side of the car. His voice quivered. "And where are... *they*?"

"I don't know," I said.

"Somebody! Anybody! HELP US!" Eliot screamed.

The fingers crawled up my neck as Eliot's voice rose in volume.

"Quiet!" I hissed, covering his mouth with my hand. "I don't know where the crew is, so let's get the engineer. Someone has to be driving the train."

I left Eliot in the doorway and stepped carefully over the couplers under the night sky. The brush rushed by in the darkness. We seemed to have picked up speed. I found the engineer sitting in the exact same position as earlier, his back to me, without even a light to help him see. I cleared my throat as I approached, but he didn't move.

"Excuse me, sir?" I said. "I'm sorry to interrupt, but there's an emergency."

I laid my hand on his thin shoulder. It felt hard, like exposed bone. Slowly, he turned to look at me. Under the brim of his cap, his face was blank, white, expressionless. Pure plastic. He had no eyes, yet I could feel him staring at me, taking me in. Leaning on the railing for support, he pulled himself to his feet in a stiff, jerky motion, his joints creaking like the workings of an old doll. I stumbled backward, almost falling into the gap between the locomotive and the Pullman.

"Eliot, RUN!" I cried.

Eliot stood still, his mouth a wide O of shock and bewilderment. I seized him by his shirt collar, and together we barged through the door into the Pullman. We raced down half the length of the car. When we reached the dining room, we stopped in our tracks. Eliot crashed into me from behind.

They had all gathered there, every last mannequin, their faces smooth and featureless in the starlight. The silk and wool of their gowns and waistcoats rustled as they formed a circle around us and began to close in, vague humanoid shapes moving like shadows. Behind me, Eliot gasped and went quiet.

This time, the fingers that tightened around my throat weren't tingly, and they weren't imaginary. They felt cold and dead...

...but very real, and very strong.

"THE THICKET"

Chase Hughes

I awoke with a start, groggy and rubbing my eyes. My blood froze when I heard the noise again, some screeching, screaming. Fear coursed through my body. While the hammock was warm, it did not evoke a feeling of safety. My bunker was a thin line of fabric to the outside. "Dad," I whispered harshly, though I couldn't see him in the utter darkness of the woods.

Movement from his hammock answered. "What?" he asked, his voice filled with sleep.

"Did you hear that?" I asked, somewhat stupidly. He had been asleep after all.

As soon as I finished talking, the sound echoed again. It sounded tortured, pained in some way, but something else that I thought of later; it sounded angry. It sounded twice more before abruptly stopping, letting the silence of night fall once again.

"A fox," Dad mumbled over the sound of him rolling over to fall back asleep. I didn't try to wake him again, though I wasn't quite sure I believed him either. I don't know how long I lay there, shivering and fearful.

The normal nighttime sounds of the forest soon returned. At some point, I drifted off to sleep.

The alarm blared, and I nearly fell out of my hammock as I woke up too quickly. Following a short wrestling match with my hammock to get to it, I turned it off. I rolled out of the hammock and took in the early morning light through the trees.

Dew collected on every blade of grass, the pale light illuminating the thousands of droplets. We were on the side of some steep ridge, just a few hundred yards below the crest. I could look out and see across the valley, still cast deep in shadow.

I pulled on my boots and sat down on the wet earth, tired, stifling a yawn as Dad heated up a pot of coffee and some water for our dehydrated food. Gone were the days of us packing in heavy cans of soups and meats, the dehydrated food approximating actual meals instead. Small luxuries that I considered as I looked on at the small fire.

"Morning boy, 'bout time you got up," Dad said, finishing the coffee and pouring it into two tin cups I had bought for him the Christmas prior.

"Yeah, yeah," I responded, rubbing my eyes. "I didn't know foxes sounded like demons." He handed me one of the cups and took a loud sip of his own.

"It's not pleasant hearing them for the first time, but you get used to it," he responded then looked behind him uphill and changed the subject. "I think we're going to dive into the dark forest today." The dark forest is what we called a small section of woods that had been decimated by a beetle outbreak before a fire had raked its ranks some years prior. It was a puzzle of fallen logs, widow makers, and new growth. In truth, it was nearly impossible to get through and took hours to cross. Dad liked it because he figured not many people would be willing to spend the day getting kicked around in there.

His theory that the elk retreated into the dark forest, only coming out for water, was founded on some experience. Two years prior, he had shot an elk there, hauling it out by himself. He had jokingly blamed me for the resulting knee pain, though I had been deployed at the time half a world away.

"That should be fun," I quipped. We both knew that it would be the opposite. The conversation died as we finished our coffee and ate the dehydrated meals. A better breakfast than our previous expeditions. In the years since I had been hunting with him, Dad had improved his quality of gear, making life more tolerable while out. We weren't the types to forego actually roughing it, and there were still some improvements that we made to make it that much less miserable.

After eating, we packed up, roped our food high into the trees, and started the grueling hike to the dark forest. While it was only a few hundred yards away, it was a few hundred yards of steep grade and loose shale. It wasn't long before I was breathing heavily and sweating profusely, bent over straining to catch my breath. We didn't want to stop for long; the sooner the hike was over, the better.

After an hour or so of this, we eventually made it to the crest, the ground leveling out to almost flat. The entrance to the dark forest stood immense before us, a thick imposing wall of brush and trees. The sunlight seemingly disappeared into a green darkness feet beyond the edge. There was a reason why no one wanted to go in there except Dad. It still surprises me that elk could silently retreat into the forest.

Still trying to catch my breath, I dropped my pack and lay down on the cool rocks. I closed my eyes, and sleep nearly took me. The need for it was a wave that crested and brought me down into the fitful state between being awake and asleep.

"Remember this?" Dad asked sometime later, the sound of him rummaging in his bag reaching my tired ears, waking me from my hollow nap.

I opened my eyes and looked over. He held out his hand, holding a yellow wrapper with thick red lettering. Turkish taffy. I laughed and was instantly up, grabbing it from his hands in a more forceful motion than I had anticipated. While it was something that I wouldn't eat anywhere else, I relished every second of it. It reminded me always of my high school years with Dad, skipping class and spending a week in the mountains.

The stuff was hard as rock and took nearly thirty minutes of gumming around before it was somewhat chewable. Dad had bought it years prior for something like five cents a pop. He had lied when he said we had finally run out, apparently squirreling some away for this occasion. I was surprised he had saved it for the intervening years, waiting for the time when we would go out again.

"Thanks for saving it, old man," I said, throwing him half of the pure yellow taffy.

"I just found it, and thought I'd bring it along," he lied before turning away and looking into the forest as he worked on a piece. "About ready to go in there?" I looked to the forest too and felt as if it were looking back, something sinister within the depths.

The feeling caused unease to filter over my body, and I almost suggested that we wait on the edge at one of the nearby watering holes but relinquished the thought. I could see the excitement in Dad's eyes. He had been waiting for us to go into the forest for a long time. I had told myself this wasn't going to be like high school where I took moments with him for granted.

I sighed and got up, putting my backpack on, and adjusting it so that the straps wouldn't cut off circulation to my shoulders. "I guess so." We started into the forest.

Dad was up ahead, fighting with a series of fallen logs, trying to get over them without snagging on any of the brush. We were both coated in sweat, dirt, and shallow cuts. The dark forest had a way of kicking your ass. It had been three hours and we had made what felt like very little progress.

Time seemed to stand still within the forest. The trees never seemed to change, and multiple times I thought we were going in circles. There was an oppressive pushing pressure as if it were trying to smother us. Sounds were choked and swallowed whole by the woods or seemed to echo endlessly as if they were mocking us.

With a clipped scream, Dad fell, tumbling over the logs and onto his stomach, disappearing from view. I rushed over, broken from my ruminations, though a loose branch reached out, tripping me. "About ready for a break?" I heard him call as I clawed myself out of a bush and onto a nearby log. I just nodded and rested my head in my hands.

He made his way back over and sat next to me, checking his rifle scope for damage. "This place sucks, huh?" he asked with a nervous chuckle. Apparently satisfied with his rifle, he placed it down and took long gulps from his bottle.

"Yeah, it seems as if it has gotten thicker in the years since I came," I said, looking around. The feeling of unease hadn't left me, and I had made sure not to get too separated from Dad, not wanting to be alone in the green hell.

It felt as if it had its own menace, that it blamed humanity on the fact that it had been decimated by the beetles and fires of years prior. I looked down at my feet, not wanting to meet the forest's gaze.

Dad stopped mid-gulp and looked at me, a questioning look on his face. He sniffed three times loudly. "Smell that?" A thin smile crept onto his face.

I sniffed as well, not smelling anything other than the scent of the decaying forest, a deep earthly smell of peeled bark and dirt. Then I caught it, the punching aroma of a feral body, the strong smell of an elk. We both looked around, continuing to sniff as we slowly got up and shouldered our packs.

Dad made a gesture with his face, indicating that he thought the smell was coming from deeper within the forest. I nodded, following as he set off. We moved slower now, trying our best to remain as quiet as possible. It was nearly impossible to be quiet within the forest, but we tried our best. We always joked that elk would run at the slightest snap of a twig while remaining perfectly still following a gunshot.

The wind was in our favor, blowing just so slightly into our faces. It would have been relieving, had it not been for the stink of the animals. It felt as if I was coated in the stuff. I stopped and sniffed again. Some other smell was an undercurrent to the overpowering stench of the elk. It smelled rotten, like chicken left out too long. Unease flowed into my stomach. I tried to breathe in small shallow breaths, not wanting to endure the scents much longer.

Dad held up his hand, and I stopped, wiping away the waves of sweat that ran down my forehead and into my stinging eyes. He pointed through the trees. "Elk," he whispered, raising his rifle so that he was looking through the scope.

"Where?" I asked, unable to see anything but the oppressive forest.

He swung his gun down, looking back at me. "Come here," he said. When I got to him, I looked through my scope, and he guided my rifle until I could see a patch of brown—the torso of an elk, some distance away. It had that light coffee color fur, a contrast to the dark brown of the dead trees around it.

I could only see the midsection of the elk. We had bull tags, and without being able to see the head, we wouldn't be able to shoot. Some would take that chance, but there was a wrongness in that which made both Dad and I uncomfortable. "We'll have to get a better angle, or hope that he raises his head," he whispered, looking through his own scope again.

We looked through the scope for a while at the creature, but it didn't appear to be moving. Eventually, Dad put his scope down and looked at me. "I'll wrap around and see if I can confirm that it is a bull. You stay here and keep a bead on it." He looked back at the bull. "I'll try and make my way back but will also whistle if I can confirm."

He headed off, disappearing quickly into the foliage within seconds. For a while, I could hear him fighting his way through the trees, but even that died down with time. I was alone, staring through my scope at the elk, yet to move.

The forest was quiet except for my breathing and the slight breeze rustling the leaves overhead. I grew bored and took my eye off the scope. The elk had just stood there for what felt like an eternity. The forest was hot, the breeze doing nothing to move the stale air within the trees.

A rustling from within the bushes sounded startlingly close by. I jumped and looked over. The rustling turned to the unmistakable sound of footsteps coming closer. "Dad? I asked, peering into the bushes but seeing nothing. The rustling continued and finally stopped. The breeze picked up and the leaves shook, making a familiar sound. It sounded as if they were laughing.

With my heart pounding but trying to ignore the feeling, I looked back through my scope at the elk in the distance. It still hadn't moved, the body in the exact same position as it had been. I wanted to go home, though that was quickly overridden by a sense of guilt. Dad was having the time of his life; this trip was all he could talk about for months. Through the scope, the elk finally shifted, but not enough to see its head. I sighed, wondering if I could even shoot an elk. I hadn't yet and was secretly hesitant to do so.

The rustling sounded again, the footsteps, the wind with the laughing leaves. This time, I was unable to ignore the feeling of fear coursing through my veins and moved my rifle toward the bush from which the rustling was coming. The forest pressed in, my fear causing it to come alive and leer down at me.

A scream echoed through the woods. I looked around wildly, feeling trapped. It sounded again, distant but not far. It was Dad, I was sure of it. A large shadow crashed through the bushes near me. With no hesitation, I picked up my things and started to run, heading towards the scream.

I fought my way like a madman through the fallen logs and widow makers of the dark forest. I was clambering over one log pile when I slipped and fell, my back coming down hard onto a wet log. Wavering, I sat up and looked around. My vision felt blurry, and a heavy sick feeling settled within my stomach.

A shot rang out, barely registered in my current state. Two, three more shots quickly joined it in quick succession. What the hell was going on? I just wanted to take a nap, the longing for sleep pulling my head towards the ground.

This was no time for sleep. With all my will, I stopped myself from standing up. I was sure those shots were coming from Dad's rifle, and I needed to go help him if he needed it.

Crawling up a decaying tree near me, I found myself standing uneasily. My feet felt as if they couldn't hold my weight, but I didn't fall again. For what seemed like a long time, I stood there catching my breath and trying to calm down.

I felt alone, but not in the comforting sense. It was the feeling of a lone animal surrounded by a pack of predators. The forest was pressing down. A feeling clawed its way into me that I had to move or become crushed under the weight of the place.

This time, I moved slower through the dense underbrush. Occasional shadows danced in the peripheries of my vision, which I did my best to ignore. The leaves laughed, and sometimes, I felt as if I could hear the beginning of whispers forming on lipless tongues. All I could do was focus on my breathing and try to remember that we were just in the forest. Nothing was happening other than a mild anxiety attack. Dad must have been spooked by something that had accidentally fallen down.

Rustling sounded near me. I immediately paused and readied my rifle as the sounds continued, nearby. A droplet of sweat ran into my eyes, burning instantly. "Dad?" I called out.

"Owen," Dad's voice called out, weak and tired, "I'm over here."

I hurried over, shaking with worry. He hadn't sounded good. I saw why when I came across him just a minute later. He was sitting down, leaning against a tree. His rifle lay across his lap, a hand wrapped around the stock and a finger on the trigger. His skin was pale on account of the blood that covered his clothes and the brush around him. I dropped to my knees and looked at him, unsure of how to help.

"We shouldn't have come back here," he said, weakly.

"What the hell happened?" I let out, a whimper against the knot in my throat. I put my hands to the wound in his side, blood leaking out. He batted them away.

His face was covered in sweat and blood from where he had wiped his face with his hands. "You have to get out of here, I'm sorry." Tears fell freely through the grime on his face.

"Calm down, Dad. *We* have to get out of here," I said, trying again to reach for his wounds. Something moved behind us within the thicket. Pointing my rifle in the direction of the sounds, I asked, "What is going on?"

"It's coming again." Fear caused his voice to falter. He tried to keep it steady but failed. I had never heard him sound like that. "Leave me. That thing will get us both unless I can hold it up for a second."

"What thing, Dad? I don't understand." My hands trembled, the nauseous feeling of extreme tiredness settling over me again. Whatever he was talking about was getting closer. Fear overwhelmed my decision-making, and I fired blindly into the bushes two times. I set my jaw. There was no way I was going to leave him. I just wanted to lie down and sleep.

He started to talk quietly, his voice just a whisper. "I ran into something the other year – woke it up maybe? I don't know, I barely got out. I thought I had been hallucinating. I didn't think it'd still be in here." A terrified sob escaped him, "I shouldn't have brought you in here. I just wanted to have a good hunt like we used to in the day."

We couldn't wait here any longer. I grabbed him as he opened his mouth to speak again, his blood warm as it ran against my clothes. "Come on," I grunted, throwing his body into a fireman's carry. He tried to weakly fight against me but was unable to break my hold.

I turned back to the rustling coming closer and finally saw what had been haunting us since we came in. At first, my brain tried and failed to convince me it was just a normal elk. It stood on two hind elk legs and had the torso of the creature but had arms that ended in hands too human.

It looked down on us from the exposed skull of an elk under antlers nearly as tall as the trees around, the tips of which glistened red in the sunlight. Its eyes were red and sickeningly wet. They seemed to glow unnaturally, illuminating the deep shadows of that forest. I screamed then, but through some miracle, did not drop Dad.

With one hand, I raised my rifle and mistakenly fired it again. The kickback of the gun felt as if it tore my wrist off, and the gun went flying into the bushes. Pain coursed through my arms and shoulders. My screams turned into shrieks as the pain collided with terror.

All my options spent, I turned and ran. With no way of telling the shortest distance to the edge of the forest, I picked a direction at random.

An inhuman scream sounded from behind us, the same as the one I had heard the night before. Rage burned within its echoes. The sound of the large creature crashing through the forest sounded behind. The breeze picked up, turning ferocious in its torrent. The leaves laughed at us hyena-like, cackling as their prey was chased down.

Adrenaline made me feel as if I were the fastest human alive, though I am sure I was only just lumbering along. There was truly no path in which there weren't fallen logs in the way, but I chose as best as I could, figuring that if we fell, we'd be falling into our graves.

The forest felt unending. Eventually, I could just make out the dull edge of sunlight. All that remained was a last row of trees guarding that dark place against the light of the outside world.

Within seconds, we were bursting from the forest into a bowl-shaped glade. I ran until we reached the opposite end of the clearing before collapsing, sucking in deep, hard breaths to ease the burning in my chest.

How we were not caught, I'll never know. I figure the Forest wanted us out, showing only a proportional amount of aggression as we showed it. Or we could have just been extremely lucky to come out the other side. I doubt that. The creature would have caught us within seconds.

We limped and fell down the rest of the mountain. The sun had set long after we reached the road. By the last of our luck, a driver passed by soon after. Dad survived, though just barely. He never did tell me what happened in his experience or the afternoon after we split up.

We don't hunt anymore, though sometimes we take small nature hikes. We always make sure to avoid the deep forest.

"A Glitch at the Tavern Obscura"

Kelley J. P. Lindberg

The battered iPhone in the lost-and-found box beneath the bar had never been claimed. Tabitha turned the phone over in her hand a few times and then scanned the sparse crowd. The rain—unusual for a Utah summer—had kept most folks home, and the energy level in the tavern had dropped just south of lethargic. Tamara powered on the phone.

Full charge. No passcode. No contacts. No pics.

She thumbed the camera to life, nodded to the other bartender, and came out from behind the bar. "Unclaimed phone," she called out to the crowd. "Let's fill it up! Give me your best 'come hither' looks!"

Tamara started taking happy snaps of the tavern's patrons, who struck poses they'd never strike sober. It was, as she'd suspected, just the thing to liven up a bored crowd on a rainy night.

Noting a surge of fresh orders and a meaningful look from her fellow bartender, Tamara slipped back behind the bar. She handed the phone to a young woman in a sparkly tank top before carefully floating blue vodka over the banana liqueur layer of a Superman Shot—tonight's special. "Take a look," she said. "Did I catch anything good?"

The woman opened the gallery, laughed, paused... then touched the screen, bending closer. Her grin faded and her eyes narrowed. She flipped through the photos slowly, finally returning to the one of her.

"That's my mom behind me," she said softly.

Tamara slid the Superman Shot to a waiting customer, then leaned closer to the woman. "What's that?" she asked.

"My...my mom." The young woman's eyes were wide now, staring up at Tamara.

A tattooed man with a red-tinged beard squinted over the young woman's shoulder at the small screen. Then he glanced behind him as if searching for the older woman he could see in the photo.

"She died last year." The young woman blinked, then wiped a tear from her cheek with the back of her hand.

The guy's head whipped back around. "Then how...?"

She shook her head, her eyes still shining. Then, she carefully handed the phone back to Tamara, almost like an offering. "There's more."

Tamara flipped through the pictures. In a few, faces appeared behind the subject of the shot, smiling. But they didn't look right. More washed-out. Pale. Faded. Like a double image on film.

But this wasn't film.

"Hey, guys, come look," Tamara said in her bar-commanding voice. The noise level dropped as the patrons turned to see what they were missing.

Several of the customers drew closer and clustered around the phone. Three gasped in turn as Tamara swiped through the photos. Each recognized someone they'd lost that year.

A parent.

A friend.

A child.

Tamara quit the bar that night. People needed to know why they felt shadows watching over their shoulders. Now she could finally do something more than pour them a double.

"REST STOP"

John Daly

Hector Núñez sat dead tired, compelled to listen to the muted argument invading his privacy as he strained to finish off the most monumental crap he had taken in weeks. The squabbling voices came from behind the cinder block wall at his back, which separated the men's from the women's restroom. Two voices: one obviously a woman's, the other unmistakably male. Some dude had followed his woman into the bathroom, and now the two were going at it.

Hector grunted, took in a breath, and squeezed his gut to coerce his bowels to work faster. "Come 'on, man, be done with me," he pleaded.

Nothing.

A thud. Against the blocks at his back. "Orr en ash'ho," said a sharp, high-toned voice, muffled and indistinct, but loud enough to hear through the wall. The woman, it sounded like.

Lifting his gaze, he translated. *You're an asshole*, he guessed.

Like listening to radio chatter returning from a fading station, he had begun to pick out intermittent words here and there. He sighed, trained his focus on the bit of silvery glimmer playing off the brushed nickel sheen of the stall door corralling him into his small, cramped space. "Wait for it," he muttered. His disembodied reflection stared back, listening for the response.

"At's u'shit," blared out, low-toned but just as loud. The man for sure.

"Yep." He sighed. "There it is."

He sounded the words out, whispering, "Ats... ats..." He bit his lip, considering. The woman's three-word description he'd deciphered with relative ease. But this two-word invective made him ponder. "Ats—That's...," he determined aloud. "Oooit... U-it..." Then it came. *That's bullshit*, he decided.

Shaking his head, he put a hand to the back of his neck, took in another long breath, held it with a groan, and then let it out into the dank air. The couple's issue was easy to piece together. She wanted to break up. He didn't.

Lowering his gaze, he rolled his wrist until the face of his wristwatch canted into the meager light. Already after midnight.

"*Ay Dios*," he lamented. They'd started up long before the hour.

Something banged again. Another muted volley followed, sounding through the bricks, but now the voices intermingled into one drawn-out screaming match, becoming impossible to make out any one word. Back to where it began.

He grimaced. Not too long ago, he'd begun his business alone and in peace, thankful for the deserted highway, hoping the late hour would keep it that way. But it was not to be. The odious rumble of the engine muscling in off the highway put a damper on that notion. The engine cut off, a car door slammed, then voices—unintelligible, raging—two, maybe three, he couldn't tell at first. A few moments later, a door outside, to the women's room he assumed, clunked open, then thudded closed. He guessed the men's door on his side would open next. Instead, the women's room door opened again, and a deep voice bellowed, one belonging to someone with no business on that side of the restroom, which was clear when a higher-pitched tone screamed back. And what started as indistinguishable, very angry words, exploded into an argument.

The voices faded a bit, and then a clang sounded. *That was a door slam.* He nodded, a very distinguishable metallic sound, even from beyond the block wall. A stall door, he figured.

"Are you yelling at her when she's trying to squat?"

He pictured the boyfriend standing outside the toilet door, jabbering away about how she'd done him wrong. He smirked. Had to be the reason, right?

"Dude. Come on. Let her pee in peace, for Christ's sake." He considered. "Has to be a white dude," he determined aloud. Always think they own their women. He let the thought fester. "Naw, can't say that. A dude's a dude. We're all assholes," he snickered.

"Fuck you," hollered out as if in response to his self-dialogue. That was the woman, high-toned and raging. No need to decipher that statement.

"*Mierda*," he cursed. "Such language."

He listened for the boyfriend. Silence. "They done finally?"

"Uk ooo tu," bellowed back. *Fuck you too*, he figured. That was the dude, low-toned, venting reciprocal rage, if not more.

Hector waited, still staring into the reflected glimmer of his stall door.

A muted shriek fired back from the woman's voice, followed by another muffled retort from the dude; returned once more by the woman. But the prior few moments of lucidity dissolved as the words of the argument became once again a garbled mess. The man bellowed. The woman screamed back.

His hand slipped off his neck and thumped back to his knee. "Should have just drove," he admonished himself for the umpteenth time. He clasped his fingers and shook his head. "Eh, truck just wouldn't have made it."

He listened. The argument continued.

"Had to hitch, man," he told himself. "Had to."

He recalled stating this very logic to Carl Brisker, the trucker who picked him up at the Maverik in Fillmore. "Didn't want to risk the drive across the desert," he explained to the trucker. "It's a good little truck, but lots of miles. Money's a bit tight until I get to Vegas, especially if I broke down." He shrugged. "So, got a ride with my roommate this far. Was going to catch a bus..." He shrugged again. "But decided to save a little cash and, you know, hitch the rest of the w ay."

Trucker Brisker, as Hector thought of him, spit tobacco into a 7-Eleven cup tucked at his crotch, a constant habit Hector noted as he drove. He was gray-haired with a ponytail and wore bib-overalls, the unstained denim over his chest a statement to his targeting accuracy.

"Glad to help out," Trucker Brisker stated.

Hector nodded. "Sure appreciate it."

"What's in Vegas?"

"Pounding two-bys. All summer long," he reflected.

Trucker Brisker spit.

"Next year's tuition," Hector added. Then he explained, "Construction work at a new casino. Better pay than anything I could find in Salt Lake."

"College?" Brisker asked.

"Yeah. The U," Hector said. "University of Utah."

"Oh-ah, that's a good school."

"Uh-huh. Expensive though."

Trucker Brisker raised a brow in sympathy. "I bet."

The ride had gone well, Trucker Brisker talking about the road, Trucker Brisker spitting, Hector talking about school, both taking turns to nod here and there or to interject an *Uh-huh* or a *cool* or a *is that right* between descriptions, until St. George.

At the Shell stop for fuel, Trucker Brisker filled up with diesel, and Hector filled up with two Micky D cheeseburgers and a large chocolate shake. Forty miles later, just out of Arizona over the Nevada border, both entrees began to mutiny in his gut. By the time the moon reached zenith, with only a few hours left to go, Hector regretfully requested Trucker Brisker let him off at this rest area, deserted at the time, to take care of business.

"I can't wait for you," Trucker Brisker said, his tone tinged with what might be pity. "My schedule won't allow."

"No problem," Hector replied. "I'll catch a ride later. But, man, you know, I gotta go."

Trucker Brisker chuckled, watching Hector step down to the blacktop from the passenger seat beside him. "I know how that feels, trust me. I been there. Well, good luck now."

"*Gracias,*" Hector said.

"*De Nada,*" Trucker Brisker replied, and back onto the empty highway he drove.

Now, here he squatted inside a cold rectangle of concrete, amidst the scree of the desert at a rest area in the middle of nowhere, in the middle of the night, shitting a brick while forced to listen to some ticked-off boyfriend blow up at his ticked-off girlfriend.

As if directed by his thoughts, the voices grew louder once again.

"...want more," the high-pitched voice said. The woman.

Who doesn't, Hector thought.

"Won't wow it," the dude said.

Wow it? Hector wondered. *Won't allow it*, he deciphered.

"Screw you," came a reply.

Hector smirked.

The woman said something finishing with "...out."

Get out, Hector nodded. He listened, and sure enough, a raging response, indecipherable but clearly vulgar, spewed back.

"This can't go on." Hector leaned forward, spread his elbows wide, clasped his fingers, eyes on the concrete floor below, and clenched. Still nothing. "C'mon already," he beseeched again. He grunted, concentrated on the task at hand, and looked directly at a pair of—*feet?*

His heart stopped.

His breath held.

He had not heard anyone enter the bathroom.

Where the bottom edge of the stall door blocked his view of the floor beyond, the concrete surface darkened with an odd foot-shaped shadow. No shoes. No toes. Nothing to indicate whether the foot was clad or bare. Just shadow—and zero sound.

He leaned to his right over the silver box covering the paper roll dispenser, studying the empty space in between the top and bottom door hinge. Dull, shadowy light filtered through the vertical slot... and... something was there. He sensed a presence under the ceiling light beyond, or just about to block the light. Someone *standing*?

The argument grew louder.

Should I say something? He wondered. Bolstering his nerve, he decided he should. "Sorry, man," he said. "They been going at it for about twenty minutes. I just want to get out of here."

No response.

Thinking he might be able to see better, he leaned further. But no—he still saw no one. He hunched forward, lowering his gaze to maybe catch a glimpse under the door. The shadow moved farther away, but not deliberately, more as if Hector himself was the one moving away. He felt a sudden unease. He shifted to the opposite side of the door and peered through the matching empty space, this one above the door lock. The light over the lock flickered. For sure someone *was* there. But again, the further he moved to get a look, the more the person moved out of sight. He felt as if he were trying to see his own reflection inside two mirrors, one facing the other. No matter how close he maneuvered, like searching for the image inside the mirror, the reflection you knew *was* there was *not* there.

"Sorry," he repeated, not really knowing why he was apologizing.

A dark flicker split the light at the door lock. A brief silhouette crossed the floor underneath the stall door. If it was a footfall, he heard no step. Then the bathroom door—*opening*? So quiet, though.

The argument behind him filtered back.

"--Oan aye," he heard. Low-toned. The man. He sounded it out in his head. *Don't lie*? Maybe?

"Ooo you," came a reply. *Screw you*, he guessed. High-pitched. The woman.

"Eave," he heard. *Leave*, Hector thought. The woman again. "Get out," the woman's voice added, a bit clearer.

The dude seemed to go silent, no longer responding. *Was he leaving?*

"Ah, shit," Hector whispered aloud, the realization of something he had not thought of until now coming to him. *What do men do immediately following arguments?* "They take a piss," he answered himself. Hector knew as well that despite the available toilets in the women's room, the man would inevitably choose to relieve himself in a urinal. Mad white dudes were not ideal to meet in the best of circumstances. But now the guy would be stepping into an enclosed space that had the reminiscent odor of a dairy farm at the end of a hot day. He knew this to be true as much as he knew it would take him the remainder of the paper roll to wipe clean before he could leave this stall. Needless to say, if he wasn't finished and out before the argument ended, nothing good would come of the rest of his night.

Doubling his effort, he drew his tailbone forward, squeezed his gut, groaned, and... it happened; one lusty burst and he was done.

Relief and a smile. He could be out in two minutes, more or less.

Hector's hand reached halfway to the roll of salvation when the woman's voice finally returned, muffled and unintelligible again, but mingled with high-pitched words that were much more coherent, "Tim, ow, Tim, ow."

A chill spilled into his spine. The dude was growling something back in repetition. What? "Kill you," Hector thought he heard. Twice. Maybe three times?

The woman's voice rose in pitch. Hector glanced into his nebulous reflection bouncing back at him off the backside of the stall door. A chemical aroma of disinfectant invaded the black bristles crossing his upper lip. Hector realized the woman was screaming.

This fact dawned on him as simultaneously a protest. "Stop it," transformed into barely intelligible syllables, "-at -ert. -awp -awp."

Hector interpreted: *That hurt. Stop. Stop.*

At his back, the cinder blocks lurched. The toilet he sat on shivered, and he cursed, "Jesus."

A loud metallic-like crash sounded, ending with a muted thud. Then sudden quiet.

He turned his ear to the wall, listening. Through the blocks came a short series of scratching sounds, which oddly reminded him of static pulsating the air above some electrical malfunction.

Then, metal shrieked. Or was that a voice? Something clanged violently, echoing loudly, this time enough to vibrate the aluminum walls of his stall. Something shattered. A mirror?

Then... nothing.

Hector strained to hear.

"Bitch." Hector heard that loud and clear, as plain as if the man spoke from the stall beside him. "Ed biss now. Ain't at right, oney."

Dead bitch now. Ain't that right, honey, his mind translated. "Shit," he said and grabbed for the paper.

A moment later, a door slammed. A door outside.

"*Come mierda.* Shit, shit," Hector said—and at the instant, another thought struck him. *The dude thinks this place is empty.* He froze his hand above the roll. *No car here when they drove in.*

He yanked at the roll of tissue and a tip tore away between his finger and thumb leaving him with an inch and a half triangle of pure disaster.

The door to his side, the men's side rest area bathroom, slammed open.

"Goddammit," a voice said. "Dead now bitch, aren't you."

Hector instinctively lifted his boots off the concrete floor.

"Bitch, bitch, bitch, bitch, bitch," the man said. A squeal, like air escaping a balloon sounded, accompanied by a pulsating tic, tic, tic, tic, followed immediately by rushing water. That was the sink; plumbing beneath the restroom had just come alive, and water gushed out from the faucet. The man was washing, although he had yet to pee.

Hector froze. His feet hovered.

The squeal rose again for a split second, then abruptly ended as if muted by a remote control, and the water flow ceased.

Aii, Hector thought. Both thighs were cramping.

He caught sight of the man through the thin sliver of space between the door and the frame of the stall. When moments before he discerned only a shadow, the man's solid figure moved in and out of the vertical line of light just above the lock, alternately blocking then releasing the glow of the fluorescents spilling from above. Then the dude stopped. The man stood unmoving, his back facing directly opposite his stall door. An olive-green shirt hung over blue jeans, and a dusty butch-cut topped a white man's cranium; the backside, as it were. His shoulders stooped forward away from Hector. *Over the sink*? Hector considered. *Inspecting himself in a mirror*? Hector shifted out of view. If he could see the man, the man could see him.

The remaining light above the lock vanished. Hector watched. Black filled the space. It flickered–amber, black, amber, black—then light returned, and this time the remaining shadow vanished. Not five seconds later, Hector heard the man pissing. "Smells like a fucking shit hole in here," the dude groaned.

At that moment without warning Hector's bowels decided they'd had enough freezing in place for the day and gave out one last blast of rebellion.

Hector could have cried.

"Motherfuck!" the man said. "Mother cock-sucking fuck," he added as if pronouncing a name of a hated friend. "Who's in here?"

Half a dozen scenarios raced through Hector's mind. Each one ended with him laid out on a urine-soaked restroom floor, with either a cracked head or a bloody exit wound.

Hector was not a big man and mostly because of this considered himself a Walking Away Man. His own term. "Better to leave with teeth than stay to give them away," he had once said to a workmate during a night out on the town. But no walking away from this one was there. The situation struck him as almost comical. Hell, it *was* comical. He was SOL, as the gringos liked to say. *Shit out of luck*.

The light running up and down either side of the door in front of him suddenly vanished and then reappeared. The man had just passed by his stall. A thought sprang to him. The doorway to the outside was at the moment, unobstructed.

Act now, he thought. *Don't think. Act.*

He did.

Hector seized the back belt loops of his jeans and together with his boxers yanked them up to his waist over the stink that remained, zipping up as quickly and as best he could, praising God he was not wearing Levi's button-flys. His only real thought as he maneuvered was, *I wish I could finish wiping my ass.*

"Where you at?" the man wailed, and the stall door at the back wall to his right crashed open.

Hector leaped forward, pinched the slide of the door lock between his knuckles, slid the latch, and plastered his back to the side panel of the stall, slamming his spine up to the metal as if against an outfield fence to make a warning track catch.

How many stalls were there before his?

Disregarding this thought, he pulled the door inward, turned an awkward pirouette to the outside, and in three steps was to the bathroom door separating him from the night.

"Bastard!" he heard behind him.

Having only a split second to glance back, he saw the man, a white dude all right, turning from the last stall, a red face twisting with rage. The green shirt was splattered with dark, nearly black, splotches of abstract art. *Blood?* The man's glaring eyes bore down on him with a look of pure hate.

Hector glanced away and was out the door, took three more strides, and ran smack into someone standing directly outside.

She stood maybe an inch taller than him. She had stringy blonde hair that fell over thin shoulders just above small flat breasts with nipples erect behind a sheer pinkish tank top. Her arms were covered in tattoos. And blood.

Hector noted the left side of her head was a bit shinier than the right. Her scalp above the ear glistened.

She nodded down at him. Blood-matted hair parted over a grotesque head wound.

On instinct, Hector grabbed her wrist. "Come. He is inside. *Sígueme.*" He pulled and she did not budge. In fact, it felt as if he were trying to dislodge a statue. The strength of her stance was inhuman. "*Da prisa*," he said. "Hurry."

At that moment, the bathroom door burst open, and the white man stomped into the star-filled night. Hector scooted to the side, wanting to bolt, but unwilling to leave the woman behind.

The dude was big. He glared at Hector and smiled.

Fronting Hector was the restroom, bathed in amber, lit only by the suspended lamps atop the rest area light poles. The walkway forked, one side to the women's, the other to the men's. The man stepped ahead, blocking any retreat where the forks merged.

Then the dude noticed something else. The woman behind Hector stepped out of the shadows onto the concrete walkway.

"You leave her be, man." Hector bent down and picked out an egg-shaped stone among the border of rocks that lined the pea gravel. Not huge, but big enough, he thought.

The white dude's mood immediately changed. From the anger of a rushing bull, Hector watched his expression remold to an unmoving waxen cast of bewilderment. The dude stared—not at Hector hefting the projectile, but directly at the woman standing at his side. Even in the dark, Hector saw the color drain from the man's face.

"Mattie?" the man questioned.

The woman approached him, stepping past Hector, slowly, smiling.

Another movement caught the man's eye. Hector's as well. Beyond the path where he had gathered the stone, another figure emerged from the shadows and stepped out onto the walkway. A second woman now stood beside the first.

Her footfall was silent.

Hector recoiled. Her eyes were a cloudy and grayish mass of pupil-less sight. Purple and yellowish lines encircled her neck.

"Hello, Timbo," she said.

The man stared at her. "Patricia?" he said. "What the hell?"

"No," said the first woman. "Not hell yet. Not until we have had a turn."

From the darkness blanketing the path beyond the fork to the women's end of the restroom, two more figures stepped forth. The white dude glanced around. Hector saw two women, both with large blood-oozing holes below their ribs, as round in circumference as the poker end of a stick. Both had faces spread wide with very unhealthy grins. The blonde-haired woman, Mattie, spoke. "The girls and I thought we would give your latest conquest a little send-off party." She glanced toward the cinder block structure behind him. "Join us, Susan."

Into the cascading light, from between the two new unnamed figures, stepped a fifth woman.

Timbo, as Hector thought of the man now, lifted a hand and pointed, his expression one of complete confusion. His forefinger wavered as he backed away, knuckles locked in a strange backward curve. His bottom lip see-sawed up and down, but no words came out. The fifth woman strolled up the walk to stand beside Mattie. Hector saw she had a matching head wound, bloody and grotesque. Jutting out from behind her ear, a fragment of reflecting glass protruded. A shard from a mirror, he realized.

Hector stood immobile, staring. None of them seemed the slightest bit interested in him. The man she called Timbo turned in panic from the men's room walkway and ran right into Hector. One of the two nameless women grabbed his shirt from behind, and Timbo's face fell level with Hector's as he was yanked to a stop.

"Help me," he said.

Hector cringed, staring back into the dude's anxious-eyed growing awareness. "*Mijo*," Hector shook his head, hearing unmasked pity in his feeble tone, unable to manage anything more. That was about the stupidest thing he had been asked in a long time.

Susan stepped up to Hector's side. "It looks as if my man has been cheating on me." She reached up and plucked the mirror shard from her temple and held it up, frowning at her splintered reflection. "Seems he's done this before."

The blonde, Mattie, turned to Hector. "We all are going to have a little party with Timbo here." Turning back, she motioned with a grey fleshy hand. The other of the two unnamed women stepped up to Timbo. Spidery fingers at his back curled around the denim waistband encircling his jeans.

"Susan?" Timbo implored. But before he could manage another word, one of the four hands that held him lifted from his waist and clamped over his mouth, silencing his voice. By his new expression, Hector determined the woman's grip was anything but weak.

"Which side?" Patricia asked. She stepped up to join the big man with frightened eyes. Now completely bathed in light, Hector saw that the side of her chest displayed a gaping concave dent spreading wide over two exposed ribs, and—Hector could not look away—hanging, stringy, yellowish entrails.

"The women's, of course," Mattie answered.

"May I have the first go?" Susan asked.

"Of course, dear," Mattie said. "The last to die always gets the first turn."

Hector stared slack jawed. Susan's was the woman's voice he had heard through the cinder block walls. The voice that had ended in a scream.

Mattie chuckled. "Close your mouth," she said. Her lips parted, separating malevolently. "You'll catch flies."

Despite his disbelief, he addressed her. "I thought you... I thought he... I thought it was you he attacked—"

"No," Mattie cut him off. "You heard Susan. She died while you were taking a crap."

Hector winced. *Hers were the silent footfalls outside his stall*, his inner voice told him.

The woman turned without further comment. She stepped past him toward the captive Timbo.

The two nameless women Hector had not been introduced to held tight to Susan's assailant. Between them, Timbo locked wide, pleading eyes with Hector, unable to break free, though struggle he did.

Mattie nodded as she approached them. "The last to die always gets the first turn. More immediate anger. The first to die, however..." She paused in front of the man. Hector understood that he was no longer a part of this conversation. "The first to die," she repeated, "me that is—has more time to think of the punishment, and I hear it is a bit more fun to watch."

All the women chuckled. The sound they made was to Hector like dried leaves catching a flame.

Placing a delicate, long-nailed finger gently on Timbo's chin, Mattie said, "Time is different on our side. Over here, Susan has been deceased for a long while. On your side, it appears she just passed."

Hector glanced at the others, then back to Susan.

She winked at him as she passed. "Thank you for detaining him." Then with a motion hidden in swiftness, her hand shot out and grabbed Timbo's crotch.

Hector's knees buckled. He dropped to a crouch, clenched fists glued to his chest, thighs together. How he kept himself upright, he did not know.

Timbo screamed.

"Come, my darling. We all want to have a turn at this manhood of yours. Didn't you always want this?" With that she stepped toward the restroom door, dragging Timbo by... *by what*? Hector wondered. *By the balls*, he wanted to say but kept silent.

As a group, the three lifted the dude completely free of the sidewalk and, followed by Patricia, pulled him through the doorway into the women's restroom and out of sight. Timbo screamed again. The sound was muffled from within the cinder block structure.

The last in line, Mattie, turned back, her cool cloudy eyes on him, a disgusted look aimed his way. She gave Hector a long, chilling, dead-eyed stare. "You should go in there and clean yourself up. You stink."

"The Ghost of Montezuma Canyon"

S. M. Harmon

The hike to the Montezuma Canyon Archaeological Field School was hard, even though it was mostly downhill. Marcus Kent grumbled a little, blaming this extra hardship on that stupid ancient SUV and Mr. Brewster's obvious lack of driving skill. He heard his classmate, Terrell, stumble a couple of times, and the teenager smiled to himself. 'Too klutzy to stay on his feet,' he thought.

"The Ancestral Puebloans took advantage of their natural surroundings and built many of their structures into the cliff faces," said Mister Brewster, pointing out the ancient granaries built into the canyon walls where wind and time had carved out huge cavities in the rust-colored sandstone and limestone. The other kids listened and gawked. Marcus thought he saw what looked like a person in one of them, and he blinked. There was nothing there.

The dirt road was rocky and washboarded, but the group arrived at the bottom of the canyon and the field school without incident. A small grove of cottonwood trees near a dried-up stream bed encircled the camp, almost as if protecting it. The large Quonset hut situated near the middle of the grove displayed a sign over the door in white lettering inlaid on a brown background that said, "University Archaeological Field School, Montezuma Canyon."

The cotton on the ground was so thick that it looked like snow. Only the temperature and the greenery betrayed the true nature of the white blanket. A clearly marked fire pit was nestled in the ground a dozen yards from the opening to the Quonset hut. Marcus looked around. The canyon walls surrounding the grove towered over the tops of the cottonwood trees, making Marcus feel almost trapped. Several naturally formed caves in the canyon walls reminded him of the large cavities in people's teeth that his dad had shown him online to try and get him to brush and floss regularly. It hadn't worked.

Mr. Brewster called out to get the group's attention. "As you can see, there's a lot of cotton on the ground. This is an extreme fire hazard. The slightest spark could send this whole grove up in flames. The only place we are allowed to have the fire is in the fire pit. Drop your packs inside. You can unpack later. Then go collect the cotton from the area and put it in that bin over there so we can use it for tinder." Craig Brewster fumbled in his pocket for a set of keys and proceeded to unlock the large wooden door.

By the time the kids were done clearing the area, Mr. Brewster had placed a large amount of tinder, kindling, and firewood in the pit. "If you guys are finished, you can set up your bedrolls. There are foldable cots you can use to bed down for the night," he continued as they grabbed their packs and filed in. "Inside those closets, you'll find blankets and pillows to make a bedroll with. There's a partial divider between the back and the front of the hut. The area behind the divider is for the girls, and this side is for the boys. Outhouses are behind the hut, over by the trees."

"How come there's more room on the boys' side?" Holly asked, grumbling.

"Maybe because there's only two of you and four of us and you take up less space?" Marcus said, his voice dripping with sarcasm.

"Yeah, yeah, we all know you're smart, so shut up," Terrell muttered, making a rude gesture at him.

Marcus glanced at Terrell with a smirk. "You sure you want me to be quiet, 'bro'? Maybe if *you* shut up, you might learn something from me."

Casey looked over at Terrell and saw the boy's fists begin to curl. "Forget about it," he whispered. "Marcus is a legend in his own mind." Terrell only grunted, fluffing up his pillow for later, but he gave Casey half a smile.

With the sleeping arrangements sorted out, the kids looked around for Mr. Brewster. They found him outside, lighting the fire in the pit. He glanced up as they approached. "I used the landline to call for a tow. They should be here tomorrow morning around nine. I'm sorry about the unexpected overnighter in the canyon, but I called your parents to let them know the situation so they won't worry. Once they tow the SUV back to town, they should be able to fix it by afternoon. There's MREs in the cabinets inside the Quonset hut. We usually re-stock before we leave in the spring, so they should still be in good shape. Just go grab whichever one you think you might like and come back to the fire. If you lay them out on the hot rocks, they'll be warm in about five or ten minutes, and then you can eat them. Now that it's getting dark, we should eat and hit the rack. If you want, I can tell you a few stories about this place while we eat."

Marcus trudged over with the others to the cabinets which contained the "meals ready to eat." He grabbed one that said "Chicken à la King," and opened it immediately, being too hungry and impatient to wait. The 13-year-old soon discovered that "meal ready to eat" were the three biggest lies the food manufacturer had ever told. He took one bite of the cold, gritty stew and almost gagged. Setting the packet of sludge aside, he rifled through the rest of the meal. He discovered a packet of peanut butter which they had somehow managed not to screw up. At the bottom was a wafer perforated into four sections. He supposed that was the cracker that the peanut butter was supposed to go on. He clumsily spread the peanut butter over the "cracker" and took a tentative bite. The peanut butter was okay, but that cracker must've been made of pressed cardboard. He threw most of his meal in the trash and rinsed the taste out of his mouth with bottled water.

Looking around, Marcus noticed that the other kids had waited and warmed, then wolfed down their meals and were making their way to the campfire and chatting amongst themselves. He chose a well-worn log that had been placed, along with similar logs, in a circle around the fire pit. His log remained unoccupied as the others moved away from him. What did he care? They were all morons anyway. He preferred his own company.

The fire blazed brightly, beating back the surrounding darkness as crickets chirped loudly throughout the grove. Mr. Brewster stood up from the log he had been sitting on and began to speak. "I'm proud of you guys for handling this unexpected difficulty so well. Especially when we have to sleep in a canyon that is supposed to be haunted." Laurie Brock's eyes widened at that last word, and Marcus rolled his. Mr. Brewster continued. "Now, before you all start thinking Mr. Brewster has lost it, listen to what happened to me three years ago in this very spot."

The field archaeologist looked around at his charges and spoke again, leaning forward as he told his tale. "Three years ago, I was up here by myself prepping the field school for the next group of archaeology students from university. I had just made a campfire like this one and was enjoying some pork and beans when the air got suddenly cold. I didn't think anything of it at the time because the weather around here can be unpredictable this time of year. Suddenly, a mournful wail, almost too quiet to hear, echoed off the canyon walls."

Craig Brewster's voice dropped to a whisper. "It almost sounded like a woman weeping. I knew it couldn't be, because I was the only person up here, and the students wouldn't be here until the next week. I gotta tell you, after two or three of those cries, I was a little on edge. I grabbed a flashlight, made sure my gun was secure, and set out to try and find the source of the cries. Maybe a hiker had gotten lost and needed my help. It could also have been a wild animal. Coyote and cougar cubs make a very similar sound when they are crying for food. I un-holstered my gun in case mama cougar or mama coyote was nearby. The full moon was bright that night, so I didn't need my flashlight. As I slowly made my way towards the canyon wall, the sound got louder. My heart was thudding in my chest. I rounded a bend and started to think that I was going crazy. About fifty yards ahead of me, there was a green light shining among the scrub brush. I couldn't turn back, even though I was getting more and more scared. I just had to know what it was. I kept creeping forward, my eyes fixated on that green glow until I got close enough to make out human features. The figure of a woman met my gaze, her shoulders shaking in deep, wracking sobs. A small pile of stones lay before her. 'Are you okay?' I heard myself say, my voice shaking just a little bit. She was only five feet from me. I know what I saw. And I tell you as I am standing here, that when she heard my voice, she stood up, looked sadly at me, then pointed to the pile of stones and said something in a language I didn't understand. I pulled out my flashlight and turned the bright beam onto the pile of stones. Immediately, her face grew longer and less human. Anger flared in her eyes, and green fire shot from her nostrils and her open mouth! The skin peeled back from her face, and the specter lunged at me as though I were the cause of her grief. I stumbled backward, dropping my flashlight, and ran back toward the camp at a full sprint. My lungs burned, but I didn't dare stop. I could hear her shrieking behind me in her strange tongue, growing ever closer! She was gaining on me!"

Holly and Laurie, the two girls in the group, huddled together, trembling, their fearful wide eyes riveted to Mr. Brewster's face. The other boys shifted in their seats uncomfortably, not wanting to admit they were scared but not wanting to miss the end of the story. Marcus looked at them all, his lip curling into a disrespectful sneer. Mr. Brewster caught the look and raised his eyebrow, but he said nothing about it and continued his story without missing a beat.

"I didn't dare look behind me, because that would slow me down and she would get me! I was fifty yards from the Fieldhouse, and I could feel her cold breath on the nape of my neck! Her shrieks grew wilder and less human in my ears. I felt her hand brush against my shoulder, and I wrenched away before she could get a grip. With a last burst of speed, I jumped inside the Quonset hut and slammed the doors, locking them behind me. I could see the moonlight filtering in through the windows. I half expected to see her face at one of them, but nothing appeared. The shrieking slowly turned back into sobs and then silence. I didn't sleep much that night. I went outside the next morning at first light. The camp looked as peaceful as a graveyard. I made my way back to where I had seen the unearthly vision. All I found was a small pile of stones. I knew better than to touch them. They were obviously a tiny grave, possibly that of a child." He sat down and took a long thoughtful sip on his mug of coffee. "Never seen anything like it, before or since, and I never want to. It might have been the grave of a pioneer child, but from what I saw of the woman's dress and her speech, my guess is that she was Ancestral Pueblo. He poured the rest of his coffee into the fire.

"Mr. Brewster," Laurie's voice was barely above a whisper, and she shook like a leaf. "Are we safe out here? Shouldn't we go into our Quonset hut and lock the door behind us? What if she comes back?"

Marcus's peal of laughter startled them all. "You gotta be kidding me!" Six sets of eyes focused on him. "You actually believe that stuff? There's no such thing as ghosts! Look at you, all scared, like you're about ready to cry." He laughed derisively.

Holly stood up. "Just because you haven't seen it doesn't mean it's not true," she said coldly and then turned her back on him and walked toward the Quonset hut. "Come on, Laurie, I'm not feeling very sociable right now." Laurie followed her, looking around nervously.

Terrell glared at Marcus. "Why you gotta be like that?" he growled. "We were all havin' a good time, and you gotta mess it up and get everybody mad!"

"No offense is given where none is taken," Marcus replied, not bothering to disguise his disdain. "You want to get offended, that's not on me. It sounds like a 'you' problem."

"There are more things in heaven and earth, Horatio, than are dreamt of in your philosophy," Mr. Brewster interrupted, trying to de-escalate.

Marcus just looked at him. "Shakespeare? Really? I'm supposed to be all polite and walk on eggshells just because a bunch of brats get their panties in a bunch over a stupid ghost story? Come on, Mr. Brewster! You know you made that up."

The archeologist stood up, his eyes smoldering with anger. "Are you calling me a liar, kid?"

Marcus didn't take the hint. "Show me one shred of evidence that ghosts are real, and I'll shut up. I'll even apologize to everybody!" His face reflected a mask of defiance in the firelight.

Brewster didn't budge. "I think you should get some sleep, Mister Kent, before things get out of hand," he stated with quiet authority.

Marcus rolled his eyes. "Whatever," he said. "I can see nobody here's interested in an opposing viewpoint." Not waiting for an answer, he got up and walked to the boy's side of the hut. It didn't take him long to fall asleep once he got into his sleeping bag.

A faint cry woke him from his sleep. The dark interior of the hut was only disturbed by a shaft of bright moonlight angling in through the window. The sounds of faint snoring told him everybody else was asleep, including Mr. Brewster. He was about to close his eyes when he heard the cry again, a little louder. He thought about Mr. Brewster's story. This didn't sound like a woman, though, but more like a baby. He quietly got out of his sleeping bag and put on his shoes and socks. The air was chilly, so he put on his jacket as well, glad that he had not bothered undressing earlier.

Grabbing a flashlight, he quietly crept out of the Quonset hut so as not to wake the others. A faint green light emanated from one of the caves in the canyon wall. He remembered Brewster's ghost story. Somebody was playing a prank, and he was going to find out who. The full moon cast dark shadows from the cottonwood trees but bathed the surrounding walls of the canyon with light. He headed towards the glowing cave.

After a short climb of about forty vertical feet, taking advantage of natural hand and footholds in the rust-colored sandstone, he reached the mouth of the cave. As he crossed the threshold, the noise abruptly stopped. As the cave was shallow and the moon at a low angle in the sky, there was plenty of light even towards the back of the cave. It was small, with an opening about the size of a double doorway but opening into a larger room about twice the size of his parents' bedroom. Half of the ceiling appeared black as if someone had painted it, but the other half of the ceiling showed bare rock. The beginnings of a wall of stones rose from the cave floor about a foot high, under the blackened section of cave roof. Remembering from his archaeology book, and Mr. Brewster's comments about Ancestral Puebloans during the hike, Marcus guessed that somebody had started building either a granary or a house in this cave.

The boy looked at the other side of the cave where the roof was bare, noticing a large pile of rubble on the cave floor beneath it. "Looks like part of the roof caved in, and whoever was building here abandoned the project," he said to himself. A faint reflected gleam near the beginnings of the wall caught his eye, and he went over to look. "An obsidian arrowhead!" He stuffed the souvenir in his pocket and excitedly began looking around. Further down, where the half-constructed wall met the cave wall, he found a dried cob of half-eaten corn. Marcus hopped over the man-made wall, looking for more treasures, and froze. A pale, white, round object was visible in the moon's shadow on the wall. He turned his flashlight on, and his blood went cold. The piercing white light revealed a tiny skeleton, perhaps eighteen inches from head to toe. The tiny arms stretched out from the body and rib cage, fingers splayed. The temperature in the cave dropped, causing gooseflesh to rise on his skin and a shiver to run through him.

Without warning, his flashlight sputtered, flickered, and died as if doused with a bucket of water. A faint green glow gathered around the bones. Marcus hastily backed away, his heart pounding. Catching his heels against the stone wall, he fell backward over it, dislodging several stones, and landing flat on his back, the wind knocked out of him. He scrambled quickly to his feet and resumed backing away from the tiny remains and toward the cave mouth opening. It seemed to him as if the moonlight itself was becoming too dim, and he tried banging his flashlight with his palm to get it working again.

It was at that moment that a woman's voice rose behind him, and the green light gathering around the tiny skeleton began to fill the cave, competing with the moonlight in brightness. He whirled around and discovered the source of the female voice. The glowing green and translucent form of a woman blocked his exit. Her lip curled in a snarl as she spoke to him with an unearthly echo, in a language he had never heard. She wore a simple loincloth and a tattered shawl which barely covered her upper torso. A faint green smoke rose from her glowing eyes, and her facial features twisted with rage.

Scared as he was, his heart hammered in his chest. Marcus raised his arms in a placating gesture. "I'm sorry," he whispered. "I'm sorry. No bright lights. Just let me leave, and I'll never bother you again."

The phantom grew angrier. She pointed at the glowing pile of tiny bones, raising her voice as she continued to speak in her unintelligible language. She drifted toward him. The apparition's lower jaw distended down to her chest as her shrieks became louder and more enraged. Her eyes glowed brighter and brighter, and the smoke emanating from them became increasingly pronounced as she drew ever closer to the terrified boy. Marcus couldn't back up any further! Trembling with a horror he had never known, he instinctively knew he could not get away.

"Please, please," he begged, tears streaming down his face. "I'm not the one that hurt your baby! I'm so sorry! Please let me go!!"

The spirit's skin appeared to draw back from her skull. Raw green flame erupted from the empty eye sockets and the gaping maw that was her face. She raised her arms, her claw-like hands grasping for Marcus's throat. In a blind panic, he scrambled to the side just in time to avoid the specter's deadly grasp. Scrambling to his feet, the boy bolted for the exit but lost his footing on the rubble from the collapsed section of cave roof and went down hard. He rolled onto his back in time to see the crazed green apparition coming down on him, seemingly in slow motion. He screamed as blackness suddenly filled the cave, and he knew no more.

They searched for him for two hours after sunup before they found the cave. Mr. Brewster ordered the kids to stay at the foot of the canyon wall while he climbed up. It was the fourth cave they had looked in that morning. This one, he noted, was scheduled for a survey when the college students arrived. For now, it was in pristine condition. He noted the black section of cave roof and guessed that cooking fires had blackened it with soot. He saw the clean break in the other part of the roof, and the rubble directly beneath it. He carefully checked the cave to see if Marcus was hiding or trapped and found the tiny skeleton near the unfinished wall. His stomach knotted as he remembered his own brush with the supernatural. Looking down at the rubble under the bare section of roof, he glimpsed a torn fragment of nylon jacket. Fearing the worst, he began digging. After a few minutes, he uncovered a body. He quickly pulled the boy free and felt for a pulse. As soon as he touched Marcus's twisted neck and felt only cold flesh, he knew what had happened. The specter had gotten to Marcus. He glanced back and saw an older skeleton under where Marcus's body had been buried. The angle of the pelvic bone indicated a female had been buried there.

Marcus saw Mr. Brewster climbing into the cave. "I'm sorry, Mr. Brewster," he said. "I heard something and came to check it out. I didn't believe that ghosts were real. I was so wrong."

The man ignored him, looked around, and rushed over to the collapsed section of cave and began digging through the rubble.

"Hey, Mr. Brewster!" Marcus raised his voice in annoyance. "Giving me the silent treatment isn't going to make me feel any sorrier." The archaeologist continued tossing large stones aside as if he hadn't heard.

The archaeologist sighed and swore quietly as he removed a large rock and uncovered a body. Marcus drew closer, and with a dawning sense of dread, stared down at his own lifeless husk, the neck clearly broken, blood congealing on his face. The woman who had terrorized him last night looked as solid to him as Mr. Brewster. Without uttering a word, she turned her back on him and walked out of the cave.

"THE EMERALD EMPRESS"

Jonathan Reddoch

The helicopter landed on the colossal sea harvester, aptly named *Beast of the Seven*. Alfonso Klatt emerged from the chopper and stepped down onto the grated steel platform. He was greeted by a man in a tattered grey jumpsuit. Alfonso easily outclassed his host in his three-piece finery, yet it was the retired media mogul who seemed out of place, standing foolishly in his adornment. He was a cigar in a stack of tuna.

Shouting over the whirling blade, Captain Touko said, "We have the submersible ready for immediate departure. However, the controls have been a bit tricky to work out, so we're making do with a Nintendo controller."

"Really? That works?"

"No. Of course not. That would be idiotic. We have specialized equipment that's been tested to the highest standards. We have the most high-tech gizmos operating in the Pacific."

A member of the crew took Alfonso below deck and presented him with a tattered blue jumpsuit. "I'm Andrea. I'll be your babysitter. We dive as soon as you're ready, Mr. Klatt. You've already been prepped, right?"

Alfonso nodded and changed into the grubby attire. Before emerging from the metallic green cabin, he removed a frayed portrait of an old sepia-toned couple from his suit's breast pocket. He examined it closely. *Grandfather Klatt and his young bride.*

He was led through the rocking labyrinth to the launch bay. The submersible craft was much smaller than Alfonso anticipated. He looked up at Andrea. "Tight fit, in't it?"

"We don't normally bring passengers down with us. But for the price you paid—"

"It was a birthday gift from my daughter."

"Well, the credit card had your name on it."

"I—"

"All aboard!" ordered the sub's pilot.

So, Andrea, Alfonso, and two other crew members scrambled down the ladder and squeezed into the three-man craft. They sealed the sub and launched into the abyss.

Down, down, down, they went. The pilot and copilot jabbered among themselves. When Andrea wasn't pulling levers and adjusting valves, she detailed the situation to their VIP in a calm, soothing voice. She noticed how tense he was the farther they traveled.

She even attempted idle chitchat while checking pressure gauges.

"I use your website all the time."

"I know. Everybody does."

He was right. Everyone used his website. How else could his five-year-old daughter afford a million-dollar birthday extravagance?

Suddenly, they were upon it. A radiant beam cut through the cloudy depths, revealing the bulk of the wreckage of the *Emerald Empress of the Sea*.

As they cautiously approached, the opulence of first-class shone brilliantly in the splattered chandeliers.

"The *Empress* was overweight. They said she had a fat ass stuffed into her fancy pants." Andrea pointed to the expansive stern that had been cracked open like a Fabergé egg making a crystalline omelet.

"It was really something of a sight to see," observed Alfonso. The pilots chuckled under their breath.

"If only the builders had invested as much in safety as they did in luxury, it would still be a sight to see *above* the surface."

"Yes. Then perhaps my family would still be in the shipping business," Alfonso said with a laugh.

Andrea stared out the bulbous window at the twinkling seabed. "Two hundred passengers perished that day. But not your grandparents; they made it off."

Alfonso's smile turned sour.

They sat in somber silence as they neared the wreckage of the lower deck which carried the lower-class passengers. Though they were stored more like cargo than actual passengers.

The craft hit the seabed with a thud. The lights flickered.

"Sorry," said the co-pilot. "Power is shot temporarily."

"This happens when we're *overstuffed*," noted the pilot sardonically.

The lights blinked off, and Alfonso gasped as the darkness consumed him.

"Just breathe," offered Andrea dryly. Emergency power kicked in with a stutter, and a weak dome light illuminated half of her face. "Everything is okay. It will take a few minutes to jumpstart the motor before we can depart."

She flipped a switch and the external lights popped on. The light revealed a bloated green face bobbing up and down. The corpse was eaten away except for bits of hewn flesh and bone. His teeth were caked with tiny barnacles. And the eyes. *Those damned piercing black eyes*, judged Alfonso.

Andrea identified him by his weathered uniform as Captain Traynor, who had gone down with the ship. "An honorable man."

"Y-y-yes he certainly was," agreed Alfonso, sweating stickily into his seat.

"Unlike *some* people," she said sarcastically.

"What does—what does that mean?"

His inquiry was interrupted by a sharp thumping on the hull.

"Just the engine rattling," said the co-pilot.

The banging grew louder as it echoed through the tiny chamber.

"Not the engine," said the pilot. "Some loose debris must be hammering us. Once we regain power, we'll rise and clear free."

"So, Alfonso, is your little birthday gift everything you'd hoped?" Andrea asked, her face half-submerged in a phosphorescent glint.

"I would like to return now."

"But you haven't gotten your money's worth yet. We don't want to disappoint little baby Tabitha."

"Please."

Before he could get an answer to his plea, the six-inch thick front window plate began to crack. It was seizing up under immense pressure.

Alfonso averted his eyes from the slowly expanding, freeze-framed lightning. He focused on a moment from his distant past. He was bouncing on his grandfather's knee. Grampa Alfie would pretend little Alfonso was a ship on the ocean being tossed around by the great waves of the sea. "Here comes a big one!" he would say and toss the boy into the air.

The thumping resumed on the bulging window closest to him. Angry fists were beating against it. Skin crumbled off with each violent blow.

"The glass is too thick..." Alfonso said. "They can never break through!"

At the front of the craft, the captain's swollen face reappeared, grinning widely.

Using uncanny osmosis, the spectral form reached through the glass darkly, and he claimed Alfonso by the collar. Amidst a gurgling guffaw, Alfonso's depleted soul was dragged down to his watery grave.

"DOLLIE"

Miranda Renae

Nora had a love-hate relationship with her job, the smells of a campfire and fresh dirt being the love. She looked across the fire at her clients, the bright lights of their phones and the orange spikes of the flames highlighting their faces. Ignoring her, making her feel invisible. She hated that.

So she waited for someone to acknowledge her.

The guy, Jared, tapped the girl next to him on the leg. "Piper, I don't understand. Why are we doing this? I thought we were here to roast marshmallows, maybe hunt some ghosts. Not tell stories about them."

"Tradition?" Piper said as she put her phone away.

Nora pushed her dark hair behind her ear before turning to Piper and Jared. "Tradition is just pressure from the dead." It was why they were here, telling stories in the woods, after all.

Piper gave Jared a sickly sweet smile. "Besides, Nora tells the best ghost stories."

Jared's nervous laugh filled the cool night air. "Okay."

Piper plucked his phone from his hands, stashing it away.

That was Nora's cue; she pulled the doll from its hiding place. Heavy iron chains wrapped around its tiny body and knocked against her knees as she set it on her lap. "This is Dollie." She adjusted the doll's dress. "She's nothing special. Old and maybe a bit creepy, but nothing special." She rubbed her finger across the doll's porcelain cheek. "At least that's what her previous owners thought."

Jared opened his mouth to say something, but Piper beat him to it. "The chains say otherwise."

Nora stared at him through the flames, waiting for him to squirm before moving on. "That was the last owner's idea. She read somewhere that iron trapped evil spirits. To be fair, she spent her life inside a mental hospital after witnessing the murder of her entire family at fifteen."

The doll moved on Nora's lap, causing Jared to gasp, and she knew she had him.

"When the police found her, she was hiding in the closet, kitchen shears in her hands, covered in blood. She was rocking back and forth, mumbling about the doll and its nails. They found the doll on the floor next to the dead. Her small porcelain fingers were covered in blood."

Nora clasped the chain in her hand, twisting it around the doll, unraveling it. The sound of metal clanking filled the crisp fall air as she released Dollie from her confines. "They say you can still see the blood if you look close." She placed the doll back on her lap, playing with her dress.

Waiting.

"Is that it? That's the story?" Jared grumbled. "It's not even scary."

Nora shrugged, knowing what was coming next.

She tossed the doll toward Jared.

It landed in his lap with a thud. Jared stared down at it, confusion on his face. "What the..."

The doll stood up, balancing on his meaty thighs. Its head turned, and the painted eyes stared at his chest.

In a sweet, child-like voice, the doll said, "You're not my mommy."

He scrambled off the log, dropping the doll on the ground, causing it to let out a babyish cry.

Jared looked to Piper for help.

"I told you Nora told the best stories." A smile spread across Piper's lips. Her sharp canine teeth glistened in the firelight. "That's why I broke her out of that mental hospital all those years ago."

Piper moved closer to Jared, a predator seeking her prey. "Of course, she was already dead." She leaned in to lick the soft skin of his neck.

Jared didn't move, his face frozen, eyes darting back and forth, looking for an exit.

"A ghost telling a ghost story." Piper moved closer, licking her lips. Excitement hung in the air around them. "The perfect trap."

Nora shivered. She didn't want to watch what came next but couldn't look away as Piper sunk her fangs into the pulsing vein in Jared's neck.

He screamed, and Nora did the only thing she could to save his life. She gave him advice. "The louder you scream, the more blood she takes."

It was his choice if he took it; her debt was paid either way, and she and Dollie were free to go.

Dollie rolled over, meeting Nora's eyes. "Did I do good, Mommy?"

Nora picked up the doll, leaving the chains in the dirt.

"Baby girl, it was perfect."

"THE INVERSION"

Jo Schneider

"Are you ready, Madame McCreery?"

I smooth the front of my glossy black dress and nod at Cody Silver, who sits in the driver's seat of the luxurious SUV. The younger man is attractive enough that even a few years before, I would have lured him into my web, but not now. Nothing can get in the way of my comeback tour, not even a pretty face and what's sure to be a toned body under the button-down shirt and fitted slacks.

Cody turns his attention to his phone which is mounted on the dashboard to record us. "I hope you guys are ready too, because we're about to drive down into one of the most haunted places on Earth."

Years of performance keeps my lips slightly upturned and my eyes a little wider than normal. I'd never done a ride-along with an internet influencer, but it wasn't any different than being on a talk show or performing in front of a live audience. I had a part to play, and I would milk it for everything it was worth.

"Over the past few years, we've experienced a swell in the number of ghost sightings, especially here in the Intermountain West." Cody takes us out of the hotel parking garage and into a sunny winter day.

Skiers and film festival goers fill the snowy streets of Park City, Utah. Their breath comes out in white puffs, and I'm grateful we've got a heater.

"No one knows why." Cody's voice swells as he builds drama. "I've personally witnessed dozens of instances of unexplained phenomena, and everything before has led to what we're going to try today." Cody glances at me as we pause for a stop sign. "Madame McCreery has been in the business of the supernatural for twenty years."

I nod.

"She's an expert, and I'm thrilled she's with us."

Cody continues to ramble as we exit the quaint town and head into an area where the mountains draw back, leaving a wide meadow for the road to meander through. He told me before we started that he would edit most of this out, but that he likes having more content to work with. So, I answer his questions about how I grew to understand I could communicate with the dead. I tell the story of my elderly neighbor who died and then came to see me before her family found her. I recount the tale of speaking with Elvis, who is indeed on the other side.

This is all familiar. I could do this in my sleep.

After twenty minutes, we reach the top of the canyon, and I catch my first glimpse of the soupy clouds that cover the Salt Lake Valley.

The locals called the phenomenon of a layer of warm air trapping the cold air in the valley and causing some of the worst air pollution in the country an inversion.

"This is one of the biggest numinous episodes in the world," Cody says. "Madame McCreery, why don't you explain what that means?"

"Of course." I lock my eyes on the phone camera. "The animal kingdom follows a circle of life. Birth, life, death, and returning to the earth only to be used in another life. We humans do the same, but we have souls." I give that a minute to sink in for effect. "Our spirits return to the earth, but so do the emotions we carried with us."

If not for the strange happenings with the weather and climate in the world, no one would have given my theory a second thought, but over the past year, I'd proven my insights to be correct over and over. "Negativity is at an all-time high. The earth is having to store all of that bad energy, and when it can no longer do so, it erupts."

Cody jumps in. "Guys, go check out Madame McCreery's social media channels and you'll see what she's talking about. In my opinion, the best one is about the Old Faithful geyser in Yellowstone. Madame McCreery felt and spoke to many of the spirits there, and what she discovered is amazing."

I'd spent the last ten months traveling the world, and in doing so I'd tagged many of the natural phenomena as numinous episodes.

Old Faithful geyser? An outlet for anyone who had drowned.

The Northern Lights? The summation of those who thought they would somehow ascend and didn't but were still trying.

Volcanoes? Angry spirits that cannot be contained.

Waterfalls? The weeping of every mother who has lost a child.

"Madame McCreery, tell us what you think we're going to discover as we drive deeper into the valley." Cody gives me a serious look.

He was laying it on a little thick, but that was his style.

I make a show of straightening in the seat and looking out the window. "Before the European settlers came here, the Native American tribes often used the area as a gathering place." I'd done a quick Google search for the information and purposely kept it vague now. "No one lived here, not traditionally. Considering there are a few rivers providing much-needed water, I got to wondering why."

"Why what?" Cody asks.

"Why this place was all but shunned."

Cody takes a corner a little fast, and I reach out to steady myself against the door. During our descent, the wispy soup around us has thickened. It's almost time.

"Why do you think this is a numinous episode?" Cody asks.

I pause, for dramatic effect, before speaking. "I've only been here once before, on a layover, but even then I felt it."

"Felt what?" Cody asks quietly.

"The weight of the world."

Outside, the fog has grown thick enough that it's difficult to see more than a hundred feet in any direction. Cody taps the steering wheel three times with his right thumb, and I know it's showtime.

I close my eyes and take a deep breath. "I can feel it now."

"Can you describe it?"

My eyes dart back and forth beneath my lids, and I open and close my lips a few times. "Anger." I leave a healthy pause between each word. "Pain. Loneliness." The last comes out as a whisper.

"From where?"

"Everywhere." I lift a hand. "The lake."

"The lake?"

I nod and open my eyes. We've come out of the mountains and into the valley which is so full of fog that it looks as if the freeway is on a road between worlds. "The lake used to be bigger. Used to be a sea." I use halting words. "Now it's isolated."

"Is that what the spirits are feeling? Isolation?" Cody's voice is laced with excitement and fear. He's a decent actor.

"Yes."

So many people felt alone. This was the perfect culmination of my numinous episodes. Those in the valley often became depressed during the inversion. This is a normal reaction to not seeing the sun, but I'd decided to frame it differently. "Those who feel alone when they die come here. To the dead lake. When there are too many to contain, they pour out into the sky."

"How many are there?" Cody asks.

"Thousands." I gasp and put my hand on my chest as I look outside. "More."

I'd gotten good at imagining the specters I described, so for a moment, I don't notice the thing hovering on the other side of the glass.

"What are they saying?" Cody prompts.

An elongated face with fangs the size of my fingers, and eyes that glow orange floats inches from me.

I blink and shake my head.

"Madame McCreery?"

The thing is still there, and it's been joined by two more. Bodies trail behind them, misshapen and... wrong.

"What do you see?" Cody asks.

My throat feels welded shut, but I manage a few words. "They're everywhere." I've never actually seen anything before.

The first apparition opens its mouth. A shriek that Hollywood would be desperate to recreate fills my skull like a spiking migraine. I cover my ears and duck my head.

"Madame McCreery?" Cody reaches out and touches me, but I can't respond.

An ache of loneliness like I've never felt before fills my chest, leaving a black hole where my stomach should be. I want to weep, but I can't breathe.

Voices. So many voices are suddenly in my mind. They speak in tones that can't be heard by human ears and dialects that make me want to throw the door open and jump out.

Cody shouts something, but I can't focus on him.

A few words come in English.

"She sees us."

"She knows."

"She can free us."

I look out the window, and now there are hundreds of the creatures. Ghosts.

But ghosts aren't real, I tell myself.

A grating chorus speaking in dissonant tones fills my mind. "We are real."

I scream and cover my face, but the things are there, behind my eyelids.

Somehow Cody's voice breaks through. "Madame McCreery, what is it?"

I shake my head. I'm weeping like a lost child. "Go back. Please."

The vehicle slows.

Cody's words to me are lost in the shrieking wails of fury that now reside in my head.

"Do not let her flee."

"She is the one."

"She will free us."

I open my eyes and find even more of the apparitions around us. All staring at me. Waiting. Wanting.

My heart pounds. Tears pour down my cheeks. Fear claws its way up my throat and comes out as a yell. "What are you?" Spittle flies from my lips. The small part of me that still remembers I'm on camera knows how undignified I look, but I don't care.

"We are the abandoned."

"The forsaken."

"The cursed."

Cody pulls the SUV off the freeway and stops at a light. He's saying something and shaking my shoulder, but I barely register any of it.

"She cannot leave."

"She must stay."

"Make her stay."

My chest heaves up and down in an attempt to supply my panicked body with oxygen. We pull away from one light and head toward another. Anything farther away is obscured by the nightmares in the sky until, for a moment, my vision clears, and I see an oncoming semi.

Whatever these things are, I can't help them. They're trapped in the inversion or the lake for a reason, and whatever that is, I'm not about to change it.

The semi gets closer.

I wait until we're thirty feet from it, then I grab the steering wheel and turn it hard.

Cody yelps in surprise and tries to stop me.

I close my eyes, anticipating the impact, but it doesn't come.

"You will not die."

"We will save you."

"You will free us."

When I open my eyes, I find that we're safely on the side of the road.

Cody screams at me.

The ghosts swirl around us.

I turn every bit of energy I have to the cars zooming past only feet from our vehicle. In one last desperate attempt to escape, I undo my seatbelt, throw my door open, and stumble into traffic.

Tires squeal.

Metal crunches.

Glass shatters.

I feel nothing.

"KIDDIELAND"

Bryan Young

The woods at night were scary enough on their own, they didn't need an abandoned hellscape like Kiddieland in the middle of them. And I certainly didn't need to be heading there, armed only with my backpack full of nothing useful— a flashlight and the kitchen knife I stole from home before I left.

I didn't know what I needed the knife for, but Alyssa assured me I'd need it. At least, if I wanted to end the bullying I had been enduring at school for the last year. I just knew that Alyssa cared about me, and she'd never been wrong when it came to encouraging me to do the right thing.

"Meet me at my secret place tonight," she'd told me before disappearing out my bedroom window. "And bring the knife."

She'd promised all my troubles with Brand would end, and frankly, that was what I wanted most. He made my life at school hell every day. I just didn't know if the cost—a trip to Kiddieland at night—was worth it.

I'd been there only once before, during the day. It gave me the absolute creeps. Around since the '40s, it was abandoned in the '70s after a kid died in the Gingerbread House, a dark ride full of dolls that recreated scenes from famous fairy tales. It was in the Hansel and Gretel room where the kid fell out of the car, and their head was crushed beneath the next vehicle. Like a watermelon, my mom told me once. Just... splat... brains everywhere.

For reasons I didn't understand, Kiddieland was Alyssa's secret spot. She *liked* going there. And this was where, somehow, I was going to get Brand to leave me alone.

None of it made sense.

But I trusted her.

The back way to Kiddieland, through the woods, felt more treacherous and scarier than taking the crumbling road that went out there, but it took longer. I was too young for a driver's license anyway, so through the woods I went. The flashlight, its tight yellow beam shining a spotlight just ahead of me, kept me from breaking my neck and tripping over roots and branches.

I kept my earbuds out. I didn't want something to creep up on me. Anyway, everyone swore this place was haunted.

Why *wouldn't* that kid who died haunt the place? But there were rumors—there were always rumors—that others had died there, too. Like that hiker that got lost and took shelter in the Gingerbread House. Teenagers stumbled on the corpse months later. Or the stories of the murders that gave rise to rumors of the Gingerbread Killer.

There were a dozen kids over the years that had disappeared in the woods. Search parties were called. Kiddieland was obviously searched, and they never found any evidence they'd died there. But that's what all the kids said.

Of course, we did.

There were always stories of a murderer that would lure some unsuspecting kid out to Kiddieland and kill them just to eat them.

Most, myself included, thought that story was just a tall tale told to keep kids away from visiting the terrifying ruins. But there was always truth to every story, some small kernel where it started.

As for Kiddieland, there were parts that had been left abandoned but looked weirdly pristine, and there were other parts of the park that had been completely destroyed, looted, and tagged up with spray paint.

Except for the Gingerbread House.

That one, they left alone.

Thinking too hard about that place made me feel like a hand was crawling across my back, and I had to think of something else.

By the time I reached the edge of the park and the stone retaining wall meant to keep me out, slicked over in green moss and long tendrils of ivy overgrowth, I'd slowed to a shuffling walk.

I didn't want to go in.

On top of it being creepier than all reason, Alyssa implied Brand would be there. Brand was the kind of kid who'd kick my ass if he saw me. Add the terror of being in Kiddieland at night, and he was likely going to be eager to hit me and run.

Not wanting to go inside was a rational response rooted deeply in self-preservation. I hadn't made it to twelve by making stupid decisions.

At least not when it mattered.

But I was still twelve.

Stupid decisions are kind of our thing, right?

I put the end of the flashlight in my mouth and tightened my backpack straps before finding my grip on the wall.

In the growing darkness, I tugged on a vine, testing its strength. That would make for the easiest climb, and I could just scramble up the side like Robin up a Bat-rope. Drooling all over the end of the flashlight, almost gagging on it, I took it out of my mouth and swept it around, looking for the best spot to climb up. Gripping the thick, ropy vine tightly, I put the flashlight back in my mouth.

I slowly shifted my weight from the ground to the wall, climbing up one foot at a time.

It seemed to work, and I got halfway up before I got scared and thought I was going to fall. Then I dropped the flashlight, leaving me in the long shadows of the leaves.

Fortunately, it was only an eight-foot-high fence, so I dropped back to the ground and picked up the light. There was no way I was going to make it over holding it in my mouth, so I'd take my chances. Shutting it off, I unzipped my backpack and tossed the flashlight inside. It made a dull clink against the knife.

Zipping up my bag, I looked around, blinking, hoping the moon would shine through the trees so I could see something, but the only light came from the stars.

I furrowed my brow, wondering if I...

No. That couldn't be.

For a second—just a second—I would have sworn I heard the faint fairy melodies of a music box.

Convinced my mind was playing tricks on me, I tried to tune it out. At least that's what I told myself as my eyes slowly became accustomed to the darkness. I saw my hands in front of my face, but only just. And I turned back to the wall, groping around for the right vine.

When I found it, I pulled myself back up the wall, reached the top ledge, and dragged myself up and over.

In the distance, deeper inside the abandoned park, I made out the haze of lights.

But it wasn't as though there was any power to the buildings; there hadn't been an active power line to Kiddieland during the course of my entire life. A generator maybe? Batteries on lights? Maybe the light came from a fire...

I sniffed at the air and sensed no hint of smoke. Only that earthy moss smell of the forest on a crisp autumn night. There was an edge to the scent and the cold, and I liked it. It was the right weather for a hoodie.

But it was also the right weather for horror.

Trying not to psych myself up too much, I counted silently, dropping on three and landing in a crouch in a cold puddle of mud.

My feet immediately froze, but rather than hopping out, I was rooted to the spot.

The music.

I hadn't imagined it. It was even louder on this side of the wall. Whoever was responsible for the light must have been responsible for that, too. And then I wondered if all the stories about fairies—along with all of the ones about murder—were somehow real.

"Shh..." came a voice from behind me. I swear my heart stopped.

Alyssa stood there, back against the fence, ready for our meeting.

"Don't scare me like that," I hissed at her.

She stood there in the dark, her finger raised up to her lips.

"What are we doing here?" I asked, more softly than before, but she only beckoned me to follow her, winding slowly through the shattered buildings toward the light. Having her to follow didn't make Kiddieland any less scary. We crossed through the bombed-out remains of a cotton candy shack and entered a midway where a carousel stood. Most of the animals had been removed or looted, but the few that remained—a menacing wolf and a bear too large to move—had been repainted with large, jagged teeth and blood on their reaching claws.

I looked up to the mirrors at the top of its center pillar, cracked and grimy, reflecting nothing in particular, and it made me wonder about the faces of the children who had ridden the carousel in its heyday.

Were those memories trapped in there, some ghost of the happiness that such a place once brought?

I shivered and tried to forget about it.

The last thing I wanted to think about was more ghosts in a place like this.

I was more concerned about why I had a knife in my backpack and why Alyssa wasn't saying anything. Usually, she was a chatterbox, even in the tensest of situations.

And then I got worried.

Okay, *more* worried.

Maybe this was something serious.

Alyssa ducked behind a turnstile and stepped onto the track of what used to be a boat ride. The water had long since dried up except in the grossest puddles of algae-riddled still water, a haven for mosquitos and disease. Zinka. West Nile. Malaria. I'd done my research, and it was a lot. I thought we might be too far north, but images of alligators and crocodiles crawling slowly through the abandoned flume, looking for children to eat in the dark, penetrated through my bravery.

"Alyssa," I said, quietly.

But she didn't turn around. She didn't acknowledge me at all.

Not until we reached the end of the water-guided track, and she stopped.

She crouched behind it and motioned for me to do the same.

And that's when I realized we had a good view of the lights. Of course, they were aimed directly at the Gingerbread House.

Now that we were much closer, I realized that it wasn't a fire or any sort of electricity.

It was a pair of headlights, beaming two shining spotlights from an idling sedan.

The sight of the Gingerbread House fully illuminated, and the thought that there was someone in there, *anyone*, let alone Brand, sent me into a tailspin of hyperventilation.

"Alyssa, what's going on?"

Alyssa raised her finger to *my* lips and widened her eyes as though danger was nearby. Then she pointed to the Gingerbread House.

A figure emerged, tall and lanky. The headlights reflected off his glasses, sparkling diamonds in the dark. When I looked down at his hands, I saw the glint of metal.

A knife.

I realized that I'd just laid eyes on the Gingerbread Killer.

The real one.

I gulped.

We were in real trouble.

But I was still confused. Where was Brand?

Then I worried. As if I wasn't worried enough.

The man got into his boxy car. He turned the headlights off, and the Gingerbread House fell into shadows.

I heard gravel crunch beneath the tires, and I watched as the outline of the sedan pulled backward.

Had he heard us? Was he coming to look for us?

The tires squealed as the sedan changed direction, but I couldn't see where it went.

"Come on," Alyssa said. "He'll be back soon."

"What are you talking about?" My voice dripped with fear. "Was that who I think it was?"

"Yes. We just have to hurry."

"Hurry where? And *why*?"

I knew what she was going to say before she said it, but that didn't stop my stomach from sinking further into the black hole inside of it.

"We're going inside," she said.

"Wait a second…" I tried to stop her, but she was already standing.

"You brought a knife?"

"Yes."

She pointed to my backpack. "Get it out. You're going to need it. But we have to hurry; he won't be gone for long."

"This is insane," I told her, unzipping my bag, and pulling the broad kitchen knife from it. It was the one that had sent my dad to the ER on Thanksgiving, so I knew it was sharp. I had pulled it out of the wooden block in the kitchen with a satisfying *sching*, but from my backpack, the only sound that accompanied it was the butterflies in my stomach.

"I don't like this. Why are we going in there?"

"You want to fix things with Brand, right?"

"He's in there?"

"Where else would he be?"

Every bit of protest I offered was ignored.

Alyssa jumped over the broken canal boat, hand-carved with figures of fairies in its hull, and then to the ground and ran in the direction of the Gingerbread House.

Something that ate kids was in there. I knew it.

Why else would we have the stories?

The closer we got to the Gingerbread House, the closer I got to throwing up. The butterflies became hornets, floating around inside my chest, stinging my heart, and leaving that buzz so loud I felt in my jaw

.

I just put one foot in front of the other and kept moving, keeping my eyes focused on Alyssa. At least that way, I wouldn't be staring at Kiddieland and its horrifying sights and sounds.

As I got closer to the Gingerbread House than I'd ever been before, I realized it was much larger than I imagined it would be. I'd heard the owners had bought the ride system, an old haunted house ride, cheap from a bankrupt carnival. But no matter what they'd dressed it up as, it couldn't escape its true nature.

The inside was something I never wanted to see, but Alyssa walked right up the stairs with no hesitation.

"Is he really in there?" I asked. I didn't want to go in if I didn't have to.

She nodded solemnly.

I groaned and followed her.

There was still a car at the loading ramp, as though it were waiting for the next ride. But the electronics had been ripped out a long time ago. On the wall was a mural painted on cracked stucco that depicted the two children—Hansel and Gretel—heading through the woods to the witch's house. The house in the mural was smaller and fringed with marshmallow fluff and licorice. Aside from their eyes, scratched from the painting entirely, the kids in the mural looked genuinely happy, holding hands and skipping blissfully toward their death, toward the kindly-looking witch in front of the painted house, who looked as happy as anything. But as they got closer, her face snarled into something old and rotten, with jagged teeth and red eyes.

I startled and blinked, but my mind must have been playing tricks on me because when I blinked again, the witch was as benevolent as before.

The rest of the mural was inert. There were scenes from other fairytales with scenes in forests, and I wondered if the ride was more than just the Hansel and Gretel story. Why else would Snow White and Little Red Riding Hood be up there? The gingerbread exterior was just to lure kids into all the terrors of the forest.

Alyssa looked at me questioningly. "What are you waiting for?"

She stood in the blackened archway where the cars began their journey through the fairy tale forests to the welcoming cottage, culminating with, well, the oven.

"Where's your flashlight?"

Fumbling with the knife, I pulled the backpack off once more and withdrew the flashlight. Flipping it on, I aimed the beam right at the black hole. Gathering my wits, I tightened my grip on the flashlight in my left hand and knife in my right. The knife brought some measure of solace. If something jumped out at me, I'd have no problem stabbing it. I hoped.

Turning the corner and beginning our journey, the flashlight's focus dragged across the walls searching for details. The walls were covered over in trees, as though we were descending into the forest of folk stories and fairy tales, and we left the world of reality behind.

The first room felt like more of a corridor, with tableaux full of dolls on either side. This room told the story of Little Red Riding Hood, and at the end was the wolf itself, carved of wood with fur glued to it for realism. It waited for us at the end of the line like a nightmare. It had bright silver eyes that looked all too real when the flashlight's beam fell upon them. Its head—I swear—swiveled toward me, looking through me, a gnarled snout full of sharp wooden teeth decorated in the chipped red paint of Grandmother's blood.

"I'm not doing this," I said.

Alyssa turned back and looked desperately at me. "I know this is scary, but we have to. For Brand. I promise it'll be okay."

"Brand doesn't even like me."

"He's going to die if we don't do something."

And I knew she was right.

Taking another step, I froze at the sound of tires on gravel in the distance.

Her face melted from desperation to fear, and then her eyes met mine once again. "We have to go *now*. Please... Let's go."

She didn't wait for me. She just followed the track around the corner.

The next turn was yet another stretch of forest, the trees more realistic, with actual bark and fake branches stretching down from above. The scene told a story I didn't know: a bride running through the forest away from a man with an axe. When the light hit the lace of the doll's wedding dress and I saw her dead, black eyes, that was as far as my curiosity would take me. I just wanted to leave.

It was no wonder all the vandals had left this ride alone.

Despite being so far into the tunnel, when I heard the sharp sound of a car door, I knew the Gingerbread Killer was back. And I knew I never, ever, wanted to meet him.

Rushing, we took the next turn at speed and found ourselves in a generic scene from Snow White in doll form.

Snow White had dripping red cheeks that looked more like blood than blush in the dark, a victim of the woodsman already.

"One more," Alyssa said, and we followed the tracks around another corner, arriving at the fabled Gingerbread House. Hansel and Gretel dolls were huddled together inside the house, their doll faces painted in screams of terror. The witch loomed large over them, an old woman with sickly green skin and those same, penetrating red eyes I saw on the mural. That wasn't the most horrifying thing in the room, though.

At the back, sitting in front of a real wood-burning stove, fire raging inside it, was a little boy.

Brand.

Tied to a chair.

Duct tape covering his mouth.

Blood leaked from his nose and cuts above his eyes.

When he saw us, his eyes widened in terror.

"Tell him it's going to be okay," Alyssa said.

I nodded. Then, I turned the flashlight on my own face, in case he was still confused about who it might be. "It's going to be okay, Brand. It's me. Right? We're gonna get you out of here."

"Cut him loose," Alyssa said. But her direction was punctuated by a terrible crash of sound echoing through the narrow corridors.

Someone was behind us.

"Hide," Alyssa said.

Fumbling to turn my flashlight off, I ran around the next corner and froze. I gripped the knife and peeked my head around, watching Brand.

His eyes pleading.

From the terror in them, I knew he must have seen something truly awful. By the looks of him, tied to the chair and his face bleeding, he knew what was going to happen next. Alyssa stood behind me, back against the wall.

I took in a deep breath, counted to ten, and tried to stop myself from hyperventilating, but my heart just kept thumping like a drum, giving the hornets a beat to buzz to.

A whirr of motion came from the other end of the scene.

I quickly pulled my head back behind the corner.

I had no idea what I was doing, but I knew I couldn't leave Brand. With the knife in my hand I—probably delusionally—felt like I could help.

Suddenly, my fear of the *place* had been replaced by the fear of the *situation*.

The Gingerbread Killer stories *were* true. Those kids hadn't died lost in the woods, never to be found again. That guy was out there torturing and killing them. And unless I could help him, Brand was next.

Alyssa had been right the entire time, and she stood behind me with her hand on my shoulder. I looked back at her, and she looked right at me and nodded her head, her eyes wet and glassy. She was just as scared as I was, reliving all of her own traumas.

From the next room, I heard mumbling interspersed with Brad's screams through the tape.

"No use in screamin'," the voice said, loud enough to understand. "No one can hear you."

Daring once again to peek my head around the corner, I saw the lanky man standing over Brand, his back to me. There in the firelight, he didn't look at all like his voice implied. He seemed... normal, wearing a clean white shirt with a collar and slacks, as though he'd just come from a business meeting.

His head whipped in my direction, as though maybe he'd heard something, so I ducked my back, hoping he hadn't seen me.

"Well," the man continued, focusing back on Brand. "Not no one. *I* can hear you."

I was going to die with Brand. I knew it. Deep down. We were all going to die alone in Kiddieland, adding to all the stories and urban legends.

We'd be that cautionary tale for future generations.

Or I could swallow my fear.

I crept forward, taking in the scene, focusing on the man's long, jagged Bowie knife glistening in the flickering firelight.

He raised it, ready to cut Brand again.

I couldn't let him do that. Gripping my knife tighter, I took a step from the corridor, hoping he didn't hear my approach. I wasn't known for being stealthy. I was a clumsy oaf. But this time, I couldn't falter, or Brand and Alyssa and I were dead.

And I didn't even want to think about what might happen to Alyssa, huddling around the corner just outside of his sight. She'd escape, surely, and find some other kid to hang out with. It was bizarre the things that ran through your mind as you walked toward death, as I took those slow, careful steps toward the Gingerbread Killer.

As the killer dragged the tip of his knife against Brand's cheek, Brand screamed again beneath the duct tape gag. Blood mixed with tears, dripping down Brand's face.

I raised the knife up high, ready to place it right into his back. I tiptoed forward, one careful step at a time.

"Why are you crying?" the man shouted. "I haven't given you anything to cry about yet. We're just getting started."

Brand blinked.

And we made eye contact.

The man must have seen some slight shift in his expression because he turned to see what Brand was looking at.

Me.

I panicked and brought the knife down, digging it into his chest with all the might I could muster. Something cracked as the tip plunged past bone and into his chest.

He yelped, swatting my knife hand away, yanking the blade, blood gushing from the open wound.

Fury was written on his mute face, but there was confusion there, too. His brow furrowed, and anger grew on his face. "You little bastard."

I slashed at him again, dragging the tip across his face and slicing the skin away from one side of his nose and down his cheek.

That's when he came after me. His knife nicked my neck. I felt a sharp sting, and my shoulder was wet with blood, but I had to ignore that. I had to end this, otherwise none of us were going to leave that place alive. The man stepped around Brand and toward the fire. Instead of me, though, he cut Brand. Across his shoulder, right through his t-shirt. Brand screamed again, mutely through the gag.

I had to end this.

"Get away from him," I said.

And he laughed at me.

Like he didn't believe that I was worth anything.

That I couldn't hurt him.

That I couldn't win.

Like I was a loser.

"You're such a tough little guy," he said with a smile, taking another step back and placing the tip of his blade against the back of Brand's neck. "Tonight'll be a fun two-for-one."

I moved in, feinting with the knife, hoping I was scary enough to get him to take a step back, but it didn't work. He just laughed again.

Lunging further this time, I got in close enough to cut the arm holding the knife. He pulled back another step—toward the stove where the evil witch would have cooked Hansel and Gretel.

Rather than reacting in pain, he instead pulled his arm up and licked the blood from the cut. His shirt had gone from stark white to sticky red, clinging to his thin body like a magnet.

"You're gonna pay for that."

And that's when Alyssa emerged from her hiding place.

She ran at the killer like a linebacker, shoving him back and into the fire.

He screamed as he pinwheeled into the flames that ignited his clothes.

He dropped to the ground and rolled, still screaming.

Stepping around Brand, I stabbed the burning man in the chest.

Then again.

And once more.

He stopped moving. His face went slack, and he just... burned.

Then, I turned to Brand.

His hands had been tied to the back of the chair, so I cut them loose. He pulled his arms forward and took the duct tape off his face. Then, I cut the ropes from his ankles.

Brand was breathing heavily, scared. Tears streamed down his face in dark ribbons as the salty water mixed with the blood.

He collapsed forward and wrapped his arms around me.

"I'm so sorry," he said.

Then again.

And yet again.

Wrapping my arms back around him, I told him it was okay.

And that's when I saw Alyssa over his shoulder, standing above the killer's smoldering corpse.

She looked at me, crying too.

But there was the determination in her eyes of a job well done.

"This is where you died, too, isn't it?" I asked her.

And she nodded. Wiping tears from her face.

"What?" Brand asked.

"Nothing," I said to Brand. Then to Alyssa, I asked. "He just dragged you in here like this?"

She nodded, Brand said yes, too.

"Let's get out of here," I told Brand.

The adrenaline had worn off enough that I could feel my heart beating in my bleeding neck.

Brand and I helped each other to our feet, and we walked from the Gingerbread House. The man's car idled in front of the decrepit ride.

"I'll drive," Brand said.

And as we settled into the killer's car, I realized I'd never be afraid of Kiddieland again.

The car backed up, the headlights shone against the Gingerbread House, and there Alyssa stood, waving at me from her secret place. *Our* secret place.

I waved back and smiled through my tears.

Thanks to her, it was all going to be okay.

"A GOOD NIGHT"

Lehua Parker

When Med Tech Taylee Broadbent saw Maisy the cat saunter into room 143, tail high and swishing, she knew it was going to be a productive shift. Maisy was never wrong.

Smiling, Taylee grabbed the visitor log from the front desk at Shady Pines Assisted Living and flipped through the pages. Room 143 belonged to Afton Adamson. In the last couple of days, Afton had had eight visitors—her son and his family, the Bishop's wife, and two visits from Home Health. The mail log listed a package from her daughter Barbara—a small box of fine Swiss chocolates and a crayon drawing from her grandson Peter. At the bottom of the log was a note from the day shift receptionist saying she'd taped the picture to the wall next to Afton's bed. Afton's next oxygen delivery was scheduled for Tuesday, a couple of days sooner than last week's. In her med record was a reminder to check her oxygen saturation three times a day now, moving her up a level of care.

Congestive heart failure was a bitch.

Perfect, Taylee thought. *This'll be easy.*

As Taylee pushed her med cart through the hallways, she decided to leave tucking Afton in for last. She was never a dessert-first kind of girl.

Working her way through the warren of rooms, Taylee handed out little cups of blood pressure meds and sleeping aids, adjusted CPAP hoses, took blood pressures, and recorded oxygen saturations. In room 247, she changed the channel to the Jazz game, making Jimmy grin. "I used to play," he said for the millionth time.

"Yeah, Jimmy, you were a guard," Taylee said.

"I was a guard," Jimmy said, "Best—"

"'Night, Jimmy," said Taylee, shutting the door behind her.

In 153, she placed a call to the CNA on duty for a linen change and mop-up. 168 was already asleep, but Taylee woke her for her sleeping meds. Rules are rules.

Looping back through the last section, Taylee paused for just a moment outside of Eldamay Jackwell's dark and empty room. *So bossy,* thought Taylee. *A real ballbuster. Hope the next one's sweeter.*

After every room and cheerful good night, Taylee furtively patted the zippered pocket in her scrubs, rubbing her fingers against the outline of her special lip balm, her own secret recipe. *There, there, there,* she thought. *Soon, soon, soon.*

As she passed the front desk on her way back to Afton's room, she stopped to talk to Dallin, the night receptionist/security guard.

"Hey, Taylee," he said. "Almost done?"

"Almost. Hey, do you mind helping me out?"

"Sure. What do you need?"

"Room 241 needs a new battery in his TiVo remote."

Dallin reached into a cabinet. "On it."

"Thanks." She paused. "Jimmy in 247's watching the game. Might like it if you stopped by."

Dallin sighed. "Yeah, I can do that."

"He loves to talk basketball," Taylee said.

"Yeah," said Dallin as he stood. "You know he used to play?"

Taylee grinned. "Think I heard that a time or two. Take a Snickers."

"Good idea. It'll be the perfect distraction when I have to leave."

"There's some in the snack bin—Halloween leftovers," said Taylee.

"Wow. There's like a whole bag here. I'm taking two—one for him and one for me. You want one?" asked Dallin.

"Nah, I'm good."

Dallin tucked the candy in his jacket pocket. "You seen where Maisy's hanging out now?" he asked, gesturing down the hall.

Taylee opened her eyes wide, faking surprise. "She's not in Eldamay's anymore?"

"No. Moved on to room 143." He paused. "You think—"

Taylee waved her hand. "Nah. Afton's doing so much better. Besides, Eldamay and Afton were lunch buddies. The cat's just keeping her company."

"Yeah," said Dallin dubiously.

Taylee leaned close. "Look. I'm almost done with my rounds. Why don't you hang out with Jimmy for a while? Eat a Snickers and take a smoke break. I have some paperwork that I can do right here at the front desk. I've got this covered. If anything happens, I'll holler."

"Thanks, Taylee. You're the best."

"Hey, thank you for taking care of the batteries. Fricken remotes always ruin my manicure."

"No prob. See ya."

With the CNA mopping and Dallin watching the game, Taylee headed toward room 143 where Afton and Maisy waited.

In just one glance, Taylee knew. Maisy was curled in a ball at the foot of the bed, her head resting on Afton's leg. Her purr was almost as loud as the sucka-hissss-sigh, sucka-hissss-sigh of the oxygen concentrator. Taylee walked into the room, switched on the nightstand light, and flicked off the overhead lights.

Some things were better in the dark.

"Afton?" said Taylee. "Sweetie? It's time."

The frail woman in the bed fluttered her eyes. "Time?" she said. "Is Braydon here?"

"No—"

"Where's Braydon? It's late. Is he lost?" She struggled to sit up.

"No, he's fine," said Taylee, pressing her back into the pillows. "It's Taylee. I've got your evening meds."

"Taylee?"

In one heartbeat to the next, Taylee felt it. The room expanded in all directions. The walls blurred. The shadows and shapes of people started to gather around the bed.

Maisy purred louder.

Taylee sighed and leaned down. "Was this a good day, Afton?"

"What?"

"WAS THIS A GOOD DAY?" shouted Taylee.

"W-what do I have to pay?" Afton slurred. "The gas is already off."

Taylee shook her head. "I see you've got a new picture from Peter. I like the flowers." To Taylee it floated just above the middle of a smiling man in a bowler hat.

"Petey's a good boy," said Afton, her eyes wandering.

"Yes, he is. And you saw your son and his family yesterday."

"I did?"

"Yes, they came for a nice visit."

"Is it spaghetti?" whispered Afton. "Are you giving me more spaghetti? I really don't like it. It hurts my nose."

"No more spaghetti," said Taylee, patting her arm and removing the oxygen lines from around her ears and under her nose. "It's all going to be better soon." She unzipped her special pocket and reached inside.

EMPTY!

Shocked, Taylee looked up. Maisy stretched and kneaded the covers in delight. At the foot of the bed stood the ghost of Eldamay, holding Taylee's lip balm and shaking her head.

"Give that back," hissed Taylee, making a grab for it.

Eldamay snatched her hand to her chest and glowered.

"C'mon, you know this is the right thing to do."

Eldamay shook her head.

"Afton's had a great couple of days. Lots of visitors. Her family's here to escort her home—see that guy in the bowler's waving. It's probably Braydon, the love of her life." Bowler Guy shook his head and silently laughed as he wrapped his arm around a woman in a knit shawl, pulling her close. "Or not. Maybe it's Grandpa Bowler. But even Maisy knows it's time."

Eldamay held the lip balm high above her head, a challenge in her eye.

"Lighten up, Eldamay. This is no big deal. Give it."

Eldamay pursed her lips and threw an accusatory finger at the nightstand.

"Oh. My. God. Would you stop with the dramatics already?" said Taylee.

Eldamay narrowed her eyes.

"Fine, fine," muttered Taylee, sliding open the drawer. The first thing she spotted was an address book. She picked it up. "This? You want me to call someone?"

Eldamay just stared with eyes as round as saucers.

"Why do old people have so many scraps of paper sticking every which way? Why don't they just write on the pages? Is that so hard? And there's like two hundred names here. How am I supposed to know who to call?"

Eldamay crossed her arms and sniffed like Taylee was the stupidest person on earth.

"Whatever, Eldamay. You want me to ask her? I'll ask her. Afton, is there anyone you want to talk to?"

"What?" Afton asked.

"Talk," shouted Taylee. "Who needs to say goodbye?" She picked a page at random. "Blanche? Is it Blanche? How about Lindon? Bobby Sue?"

SLAP!

The address book shot out of Taylee's hands.

"What the hell? Don't make me angry, Eldamay. You won't like me angry."

Eldamay shook her finger at the drawer.

"What?"

Eldamay pointed again.

"Point, point, point. You're like the fricken ghost of Christmas Past! I don't know what you—oh. This?" asked Taylee, lifting out a box of chocolates.

Eldamay nodded, relieved.

Taylee opened the box. "Oooo, they're so pretty! Look, Afton. See what Barbara sent? So shiny. Which one? There's orange cream—"

Eldamay shook her head.

"Dark chocolate almond? Honeycomb? Raspberry? Malted milk? Salted caramel—"

Maisy meowed.

Taylee dug through the papers and picked up a deep, rich, dark chocolate truffle with a caramel stripe and a sprinkling of pink salt. "Salted caramel? You sure?"

Eldamay smiled and nodded.

Taylee held the chocolate to Afton's lips. "Here comes the choo-choo," she said. "Open wide."

Like magic, Afton opened her mouth.

Taylee slipped the chocolate in. "Heh," she laughed to herself, "works every time."

It took a few seconds for the chocolate to start to melt, to ooze across Afton's tongue and trickle down her throat. "Ummm," she gurgled and smacked her thin lips. "Ummm, ummm, ummm!"

"That's a good girl," said Taylee, popping a cherry cordial into her own mouth.

Eldamay dimmed the lights and scowled.

"What? Waste not, want not!"

Eldamay rolled her eyes.

"Satisfied? She's had a taste of chocolate. That's more than most—as you know. You've been around this block before. I heard the stories. You used to be a night nurse, right? Back in the '70s and '80s."

Eldamay hung her head.

"Yeah, that's what I thought. Can I have my lip balm back? Please? This is taking too long."

Eldamay gazed at her friend in the bed. Maisy stretched, turned three times, and then curled next to Afton, her head resting on Afton's chest. Eldamay nodded, once, twice, then tossed the lip balm on the bed, blew Afton a kiss, and disappeared like a card up a magician's sleeve.

"Such a drama queen," said Taylee. "I thought she'd never leave." She reached down to pet Maisy. "But you're a good kitty, Maisy. You can stay. You too, Mr. and Mrs. Bowler Hat."

Sucka-hissss-sigh. Sucka-hissss-sigh. The endless sound of oxygen concentrators drove Taylee nuts, an earworm that burrowed deep and wouldn't let go. She wished she could shut the machine off but knew that wouldn't be wise.

Sucka-hissss-sigh. Sucka-hissss-sigh.

The lullaby of congestive heart failure.

"Now, where were we before we were so rudely interrupted? Afton? It was a good day, yes?" Taylee asked without expecting an answer. A little chocolate drool seeped from the corner of Afton's lips. Taylee decided to leave it alone—more authentic that way. Maybe Eldamay had the right idea. She'd have to remember that trick for next time.

Taylee removed the lid from her lip balm, smeared a bit between Afton's lips, then gently pressed them together for a second or two. It wasn't a super strong adhesive, just enough to keep her mouth closed when the weight on her chest wanted her to breathe. It was nothing an EMT or funeral director would notice. After all, lips and eyes get dry with oxygen use. Taylee knew there were weirder things in death than gummy lips.

Without her oxygen and her lips sealed, it wouldn't be long before Afton's organs shut down. She would slip away in her sleep like the others.

Congestive heart failure was a predictable bitch.

Before leaving the room, Taylee made sure the oxygen hoses were tangled in Afton's fingers and lying on top of the blankets. She left the nightstand drawer open and the box of chocolates tipped and spilled on the floor. "Goodbye, Afton," she whispered. "Nice to meet you, Mr. and Mrs. Bowler. Keep her company, Maisy. See you tomorrow."

She shut the door.

As she walked to her car at the end of her shift, she popped one last chocolate into her mouth. She'd done her job. The day shift would handle the clean-up.

A good night. Death with a hint of chocolate. Not a bad way to go.

"Silo Stare"

Cygnus Perry

Driving home after a night shift
of cold fluorescent lights and dust,
I found my eyes waltzing along the
side of a bitter, bland dirt road.
Pondering the life that lurked just
beyond the horizon of the headlights,
a somber trypan light glared in
through my Scion windshield.
A beacon in a moonless night,
a lighthouse on the edge of
a tranquil, midnight ocean scene
stood staring, empty, back at me.
Drawing closer to the beam
that stalked my every turn,
its shape appeared, emerged
through the late-night shadow.
Towering above the cottonwoods
and every sparse building,
A silo, marked by an azure light
bore a presence down upon me.

Feeling its curiosity surrounding,
I raced around the nearest corner
only to find in my rearview mirror
the watching eye of the silo still.
Fading off into the darkness
of the lost off-road grasses,
the dimming spark kept gazing
as if hungry for my next return.

"The Forest Through the Trees"

Caroline Moreton

My older brother started looking different when he was fourteen years old. I don't remember how it happened. Ethan was born with curly brown hair and light green eyes, and he had dimples when he smiled. Now, fourteen years later, he has big holes where his eyes were, big black circles like they've been pecked out by a woodpecker. His mouth is a slit of darkness. It's flat where his nose should be, and he has no hair. His skin looks like grey canvas, and it hangs off his chin like sheets on the branch of a tree.

I must have seen the transition. I must have. Did I notice the darkness consuming his eyes, replacing his mouth? Did I watch the texture of his skin change? Did it happen slowly or all at once? Did he just wake up like that one day? I don't know. I don't remember.

I don't remember anything from those years. Rather, I don't remember anything from my home life during those years. I remember being at school just fine. I was twelve the last time I remember him looking like his old self. Twelve, old enough that I *should* remember everything. But I don't. I just don't remember.

I want to ask him about all of it, but I don't know how to. He's in the driver's seat, and I'm in the passenger seat. It's snowing outside. The endless fields along the highway are desaturated under the snowfall and the greyness of the sky. Our skis divide the car in two lengthwise and come to rest on the middle console between us. There's a country song softly playing on the radio. I point out some cows on the side of the road, and he stares at them with the holes in his face.

"I have a cow," I say.

It's a game we play. The first to say "I have a cow" when seeing a herd of cows gets to add a figurative cow to their pasture. Whoever has the most cows wins.

When I was twelve, I developed trichotillomania, the compulsion to pull out my own hair. Bald spots emerged, which I was bullied for at school. My parents took me to therapists, psychiatrists, life coaches, hypnotherapists. Nobody could figure out what was going on. I don't remember all of that. I only remember being teased at school. When Ethan left for college on the East Coast, I got it under control, and my hair grew back. I hardly ever saw him. But right now, I'm struggling to control my hands. I keep finding them pulling at the hairs on the crown of my head.

"All your cows are dead." The words leak out of the slit in his face. We've passed a cemetery, and he saw it first, so all my cows are dead.

It scares me when he speaks. Still. Words come out in rasping, gurgling spurts. When he breathes, it sounds like the wind whistling through the trees. His voice scares me. It creates dread in me. He's my brother, and I shouldn't feel this way. I love him.

"Damn, you got me," I say. I force a smile.

He asked me on this ski trip, and I agreed. We're not very close. Apparently, he has mentioned to my parents that our relationship is strained, and he doesn't understand why. I don't know how to tell him or them that I'm scared of him because he looks like that.

"I don't know why Carly hates me," he reportedly said to my dad.

My dad told me that over dinner last week when he came to visit me in St. George.

Ethan lives near my parents in LA, and we're driving to Deer Valley. St. George is about halfway between the two. "I'm driving through either way, so I might as well pick you up," he said when he invited me. Even through the phone, I heard the canvassy skin around his mouth flapping slightly with his breath.

We're in the last couple of hours of the drive. It's been mostly silent with only the radio quietly playing country music, the sound of the windshield wiping away snow, and the occasional cow remark.

I'm trying to keep my eye out for cows and not fixed on his hands on the steering wheel. His arms are twice the length of a normal person's, and his elbows jut out at the wrong angle. His fingers come off his massive hands in tangles like the roots of a tree. His hands rest at ten and two on the steering wheel.

"I'm going to stop here for gas," he says.

We pull off the freeway and into a town called Nephi. We pull into a gas station and up to a free pump. He opens his window a bit.

"So you don't overheat while the car's off," he says.

Snowflakes fall into the car through the open window and melt onto the black leather seat. It's getting so cold in here with the window open and the heat off. I grab my parka from the back seat and slip into it.

Some college girls in front of me are watching Ethan and smiling, whispering to each other. One of them walks toward the car. With the windshield wipers off, the glass is getting cloudy with melting snowflakes. It's fogging up from the moisture in the car. Everything outside is distorted.

She walks around the side of the car, straight to him. Because of how low the car is, I can only see up to their shoulders, but I can hear them through the open window. She's flirting with him. She gives him her number.

"Goodbye, cutie," she says to him as she walks away.

"These roads are getting dangerous," he says while we pull back onto the freeway.

He drives slowly. The other cars do, too.

I'm getting too hot with my parka on, the seat warmer on, and the heat on. I take off my parka and throw it in the back seat.

"Careful of the skis," he says.

My stomach turns. I don't want him to be mad at me, but I don't remember why.

"It's just a jacket," I say. "I'm sorry."

His head moves right and left as he scans the road for obstacles. He's hunched forward over the wheel because of his massive size. I feel so small.

"I'm worried about getting through the canyon. I'll go through Salt Lake," he says.

"Why?" I ask.

"It doesn't matter. I'm going through Salt Lake anyway," he says.

At some point, the snow turns to rain. Ethan starts driving fast again. I can hear the tires against the wet pavement. We're going pretty fast.

"I hate the rain," he says.

"It's safer than the snow," I say.

"I don't care." He looks at me through his holes. "It's just ugly and grey out there now."

There are not many cars on the road. There are a couple of semi-trucks in the far right lane, one after another. There's a car far in front of us.

"Your cows are sick," I say as we pass a hospital.

That means the number of cows he has gets cut in half.

"At least I have cows," he says.

I haven't seen a single cow since he killed them all. I don't want to end this car ride without any cows. I don't remember why it matters to me. But I also don't want to end up with more cows than him because he'll get mad.

We've caught up to the car that was far ahead of us. We're tailing it. The car brake-checks us. Ethan sucks in a breath quickly through his slit, and the skin around the hole pulls inward.

"Asshole," he mutters. He presses into the horn. "Asshole."

The car brake-checks him again, and he has to slam on the brakes. We hydroplane for a couple of seconds before he gets the car under control.

"Asshole!" he shouts.

He swerves into the farthest left lane and pulls up next to that car. He swerves toward it and they slam their brakes. Ethan laughs. We speed away. The car grows smaller in the side-view mirror.

Last week over dinner, I asked my dad why Ethan looks like this. I asked him what happened. He said, "Looks like what?" and ate a forkful of scrambled eggs.

I didn't ask him why I pull my hair out. I didn't ask him why I don't remember those years. I didn't ask him why I'm so angry and so scared.

We're pulling onto the freeway that will take us to Deer Valley. As the car climbs uphill, the rain once again turns to snow.

"Does this car have snow tires?" He asks.

"It's your car," I say.

"You're right."

His expression doesn't change. His expression never changes.

It's getting dark, but we can't see the sun setting behind the clouds, so the sky is just going from light grey to dark grey. Soon it will be black, and we won't be able to see the stars. It's already too dark to look for more cows. The headlights of the cars coming from the opposite direction illuminate his face as they pass by.

The brake lights of the cars in front of us are blurry red spots through the wet windshield. At the point of the mountain, the radio turns to static. I reach to turn it off. He hits my hand away. His fingers might have thorns.

"Let's keep listening," he says. "I like this one."

Once, when I was fourteen, my uncle asked me if things were better with Ethan. It's one of the only things I remember from that year. I remember saying yes, and I remember that I was lying. I remember that I was scared Ethan would hear me.

We're in Park City, the town before Deer Valley, and we're passing by this tree that has a bunch of children's shoes hanging on it by their laces. I don't know how they got there, but it always spooks me. I always think the children are dead. My mom said they throw the shoes there when they outgrow them.

We're staying in our parents' condo right on the ski run. He takes the master bedroom, and I take the twin room like I'm a kid again. He goes straight to the room and locks the door. When I stand in the hallway, I hear noises like wood splintering.

I don't sleep well. All night, tree branches scrape against my window. I have a nightmare that a man is walking through the hallway. I see the shadow of his feet coming from underneath the door. The hallway light is on even though I turned it off. He's trying my door knob and it shakes, but it's locked. I know it's locked because I double-checked it before bed.

I used to have this nightmare when I was a teenager. I know that. But I didn't have a lock on my door. I used to hear him coming up the stairs. His footsteps sounded like someone using crutches. I saw his shadow under my door. I saw the doorknob turn. I saw the door start to open and then I don't remember anymore.

In the morning, he tells me that I slept in too late. He's waiting on the couch, already in his ski clothes. He tells me I should've been up earlier, and I start to cry, but when I look in the mirror I don't see tears. Through the reflection, I look into his eye holes.

I go back to my room to put on my ski clothes. When I come back, he has put on his goggles and his neck gaiter. I can see through the goggles to the deep black circles. He keeps pulling up his gaiter because there's no nose to hook it on.

"I already put your skis outside," he says and then he steps out.

I follow. It's snowing really hard. I don't see my skis. I don't see Ethan. It's so foggy, I can't even see the ski hill ten feet in front of me, but I know it's there. I walk straight ahead, toward where I know the ski hill is, but it isn't there. Behind me, I hear Ethan's wheezing. I turn back and walk towards it.

He already has his skis on. He's on the ski hill, next to my skis. "What's taking you so long?"

He slides away from me and disappears into the fog.

I put on my skis and follow him down what I expect to be an easy run. This is the run we always take. It's called Last Chance, and it's a blue square, which means that it's an intermediate run. Green circle is the easiest, then blue square, then black diamond. This hill is way steeper than I remember, and it's covered in trees. I'm speeding downhill through a dense forest, and I can't see more than five feet in front of me. The fog makes everything look white and grey, and I can't see where I'm going. I can't slow down or turn because of the trees. I don't know where Ethan went. I only see trees. They are so tall. Their branches come off of them at wrong angles. Their roots stick up through the snow.

I catch sight of a sign pointing to this run. The sign says, "Homeward Bound," and it's a double black diamond.

My ski catches a root, and I slam into a tree. My helmet catches the brunt of it, but I throw my right arm forward to catch my fall. I feel a snap.

I'm crumpled at the base of a massive, twisted tree. I can't see the top of it. A throbbing pain shoots up my right arm. I use my left hand to feel my helmet. There's a massive dent in the back even though I hit the tree in the front. I have a headache. Snow has gotten into my parka, and even into my long underwear somehow.

I take off my glove and my helmet. I reach up to feel the spot at the back of my head underneath where my helmet is dented. It's completely bald. All the hairs have been pulled out. I pull my hand away. The hairs are caught between my fingers and fall onto my lap.

I lay my head back and close my eyes. This is Ethan's fault. This is all Ethan's fault.

I don't know how long my eyes have been closed when I open them. It takes me a few attempts to stand. At first, I have to grip both poles in my left hand. I look down the hill and I don't see any more trees. I look up the hill and I don't see any trees. The one I hit is the only one on the run, which isn't even that steep.

When I get to the lift, Ethan isn't there. I turn back toward where I came from to make sure I didn't pass him, but it's still too foggy to see more than five feet away from me. Finally, he emerges from the white, speeding toward me.

"That was a great run," he says.

There's no one at the lift but us. The lift attendant waves us through. My arm hurts so bad. I can barely grip the pole.

"I like your goggles," he says to Ethan. "Very shiny. Cool stuff."

Riding the lift uphill feels like being swallowed by a giant cloud. The fog grows thicker and thicker, and the snow continues to fall hard. My legs are covered in a growing white carpet. I feel like I'm being buried alive. The chair comes to a halt. It swings a little back and forth. There is no sound except the wind whistling through the trees.

I take a deep breath to steady my voice before speaking. "Why didn't we take Last Chance?" I ask.

"What do you mean? We did take Last Chance." His voice is even more muffled than usual by his gaiter, which he has tucked underneath his goggles to stay up. His holes stare into me.

"No, we took Homeward Bound."

"Homeward Bound is on a different mountain."

"But I saw the sign," I whisper.

He takes off his mittens and pulls out the map. His thorns scratch against the paper as he unfolds it. A gnarled finger points to the run Homeward Bound, a green circle on a completely different mountain.

"How...?"

I look down. We're so high up. I really don't want to be on this lift. The pile of snow on my lap is getting higher. But it's not snow, it's my hair. I brush it off, and more hair falls into its place.

"I need to get off this lift," I say. I feel out of breath. The fog is so thick, and we're surrounded by grey, and maybe that's why I can't breathe. I can barely see anything. My arm hurts and I don't remember why.

"We're stuck here. Why is your helmet dented?"

"I don't know."

I look away so he won't see me crying. The tears gather in a pool at the bottom of my ski goggles. It's so quiet. His whistling breath gets louder and our chair keeps swinging. He pulls at his gaiter. The movement of it makes me flinch.

"Why are you so scared of me?" he asks.

"I don't know," I say. The pile of hair on my lap is up to my chest. "Why do you look like that?"

"Look like what?"

We lurch forward into the grey.

ABOUT THE AUTHORS

Daniel Gene Barlekamp is the author of fiction and poetry for adults and young readers. His middle-grade ghost story "Curse of the Cat Man" is featured in the anthology *The Haunted States of America* (Godwin Books/Macmillan, 2024). Originally from New Jersey, Daniel now lives with his wife and son in Massachusetts, where he works in immigration law.

Charles Bernard is a writer who lives in Salt Lake City. He is the author of *A Baptism for the Dead* and *He Led Us Into the Wilderness* and *Spoke to Us*, among other novels. His short fiction has been featured in *Cosmic Horror Monthly, Deadman Humour: 13 Fears of a Clown*, and other publications and anthologies. He lives next to the largest city-operated cemetery in the United States, a sprawling necropolis that stretches over a square kilometer of grounds. He's lively enough company, though.

Founder of Whisper House Press, whose *Costs of Living* inaugural horror anthology is due out in late 2025, **Steve Capone Jr.** is a Utah-based writer hailing from the Rust Belt. He's won awards for both his fiction and nonfiction and is known as an RPG and book editor and screenwriter, to boot. His first YA historical/espionage fiction novel *Max in the Capital of Spies: A Max Fredericks Story* debuted in 2024. His second, *Jimmy vs. Communism*, is set for a nationwide release by Gibbs Smith in 2026. You can find his short fiction in anthologies including *We Are Dangerous* (2023, LUW Press), *Write Where You Belong* (2024, LUW Press), and *Darkness 102* (2025, Collective Tales Publishing). He's a pizza advocate, dog rescuer, and proud member of both the League of Utah Writers and Horror Writers Association. You can find Steve's incorporeal footprint via https://linktr.ee/stevecaponejr.

John Daly hails from the Pacific Northwest but currently calls home a quiet neighborhood at the base of the Wasatch mountains just south of Salt Lake City. He works days as a Building Enclosure Consultant while spending evenings with his life-partner Meg, attempting to keep up with their seven dogs and handicapped cat. They are passionate foster care parents of senior dogs (crusty old chihuahuas are always welcome) and other canines in need of rehabilitation prior to adoption. John's other passions include baseball, canoeing, and American history. But his ultimate passion is writing, having devoted years to the craft of storytelling, producing a plethora of works ranging from speculative fiction to slice-of-life adventures and, from time to time, all-out mind-messing horror. You can reach John at jaydeepub@ya hoo.com.

S. M. Harmon is a writer, a husband, a father, a grandfather, a nerd, a DM, a gamer, and many other things. This is his first time having a story in print, and he's so glad that you are taking time to read it. He hopes to get more of his work published in the future, and is working hard on a fantasy novel at this time. He doesn't have an author page yet, but he will by the time his novel is finished. He thanks his family for their continued support.

Michelle Hartman is the author of four poetry books. Hartman's work can be found in *Crannog, Galway Review, The Atlanta Review, Door/Jar, Penumbra, Poem, Southwestern American Review, Carve*. She is the former editor of Red River Review.

https://www.pw.org/directory/writers/michelle_hartman

Alicia Hilton is an author, editor, actor, attorney, professor, and former FBI Special Agent. Her poetry has been nominated for the Rhysling Award and the Dwarf Stars Award. Her work has appeared or is forthcoming in *Twenty-two Twenty-eight, Back 2 OmniPark, Bullshit Lit, Dreams & Nightmares, Eastern Iowa Review, Gamut, Litro, Modern Haiku, Mslexia, Neon, NonBinary Review, Roi Fainéant Press, Stoneboat Literary Journal, Strange Horizons, Vastarien, World Haiku Review, Year's Best Hardcore Horror Volumes 4, 5 & 6,* and elsewhere. Her website is https://aliciahilton.com. Follow her on Twitter @aliciahilton01 and Bluesky @aliciahilton.bsky.social.

Chase Hughes is a veteran and student at the University of Arizona who experienced his teenage years on the Wasatch Front. He writes in his sparse free time when he is not playing with his pets (1 dog and 2 cats) or watching TV shows with his partner. His favorite genres are Horror and Science Fiction. You can follow him at @Hugsterwrites on X.

MJ Huntsgood (any/all) is a speculative thriller and horror author, specializing in the cozy side of the macabre. When she's not being extra spooky, she's running your local D&D game or trying to complete an escape room in every state in the US. You can find her hanging out with her 18 plants, 2 cats, and trophy husband.

website: www.mjhuntsgood.com

Twitter/X: MJHuntsgood

Instagram: MJHuntsgood

Derek Hutchins is a screenwriter, director, and author of the novella *The Darkness* and of a collection of short horror stories *The Under-taker and Other Macabre Tales*. Raised in Connecticut, (the most haunted state), he developed a love for horror and the fantastic at an early age. Derek has an MFA in Writing for Film and Television from Emerson College and lives with his wife and daughters in Utah. Follow him on Instagram @themanwhoknewjustenough or (X) @derekmhutchins for updates.

Caryn Larrinaga is an internationally best-selling mystery and horror author. Her award-winning works include novels and short stories, as well as content for RPGs, newspapers, and zines, with adaptations for film and audio. In 2021, the League of Utah Writers named her Writer of the Year. Watching scary movies through split fingers terrified Caryn as a child, and those nightmares inspire her to write now. Exploring her fears through writing makes her feel less foolish for wanting a buddy to accompany her into the tool shed.

Visit www.carynlarrinaga.com for free short fiction and true tales of haunted places.

When **Kelley J. P. Lindberg** isn't writing or speaking at writing conferences, she's traveling as far and as often as she can. She's raced hermit crabs in the British Virgin Islands; slept in an Irish nunnery; eyed Mt. Vesuvius warily from the streets of Pompeii; snorkeled with sharks in Belize, stingrays in Bora-Bora, and a thousand dolphins in South Africa; and commiserated over the slings and arrows of outrageous fortune with Shakespeare's ghost in Stratford-Upon-Avon. Visit her website and blog (and sign up for her newsletter) at www.KelleyLindberg.com, or follow her on X-Twitter and Instagram: @KelleyLindberg1

C. H. Lindsay (Charlie) is an award-winning poet & writer, housewife, and book-lover—not necessarily in that order. She currently has short stories and poems in over forty anthologies and magazines including *Amazing Stories, Fantasy Magazine, Moonletters, Space and Time Magazine, Strange Horizons,* and *Utah's Best Poetry and Prose*. She is currently working on five novels, six short stories, and at least two dozen poems (although the numbers are always in flux).

In 2018 she became Al Carlisle's literary executor. She now publishes his true crime under *Carlisle Legacy Books, LLC*.

She is a member of SFWA, HWA, SFPA, LUW, and is a founding member of the Utah Chapter of the Horror Writers Association. Mostly blind, she lives in Utah with her "seeing-eye husband," library of books, and a bossy cat. You can learn more about her at www.chlindsay.net .

Caroline Moreton is a writer based in London. She holds an MA in Creative and Life Writing from Goldsmiths College. She's working on a collection of interconnected short stories based on her time living in Southern Utah.

You can find more of her work at CarolineMoreton.com.

Lehua Parker writes speculative fiction for kids and adults, often set in her native Hawai'i. Her award-winning and best-selling series include the Niuhi Shark Saga trilogy, Lauele Fractured Folktales, and Chicken Skin Stories. Her short stories have appeared in *Va: Stories by Women of the Moana, Dialogue,* and *Bamboo Ridge*, and are collected in *Sharks in an Inland Sea*. Her plays have been performed by The Honolulu Theatre for Youth.

A Kamehameha Schools graduate, Lehua is a passionate advocate of indigenous voices and authentic representation in media. She is a frequent speaker at conferences, schools, and symposiums, and mentors through the Lehua Writing Academy and PEAU Lit. When the right project wanders by, she's also a freelance editor and story consultant. Connect with her at www.LehuaParker.com.

Social Media Links

Facebook: https://www.facebook.com/LehuaParker/
Instagram: @LehuaParker
Twitter: @LehuaParker

Amazon Author Link: Lehua Parker
Barnes & Noble Author Link: Lehua Parker

Cygnus Perry is an undergraduate student at Utah State University. They have lived in Utah since they were in high school where they developed a passion for creative writing. Cygnus loves to explore the natural world and uses it as inspiration for unnatural stories and poems. For Cygnus, writing is the best way to discover the unreal and unbelievable. Follow them on Twitter @perrypianist and on Instagram @perrypurplefingers.

Jonathan Reddoch is co-owner of Collective Tales Publishing. He is a father, writer, editor, and publisher. He writes sci-fi, fantasy, romance, and especially horror. He focuses primarily on flash fiction, but also writes poetry and short stories. He has been working on his enormous sci-fi novel for over a decade and would like to finish it in this lifetime if possible. He's from southern California but lives in Salt Lake City. Find him on Instagram: @Allusions_of_Grandeur_ CTPfiction.com

Miranda Renae spent much of her childhood avoiding reading. Until her dad gave her a novel full of suspense and horror that she'd only seen in movies—but better. From that day forward, she devoured the written word; no genre was safe. Miranda spends her days weeding through paperwork. But at night, she braves the darkness of her nightmares to build worlds of her own. Check out www.mirandarenae.com for more from Miranda Renae.

Jo Schneider grew up in the wild west, and finds mountains helpful in telling directions. Goals include: travel to all seven continents, become a Jedi Knight, and receive a death threat from a fan. She's still working on the death threat. Jo writes science fiction and fantasy with amazing characters that she's not particularly nice to.

Website: joannschneider.com

Facebook: @JoannSchneiderWriter

Bryan Stubbles has published short nonfiction in *Out of Time*, short fiction in *Wasatch Witches* and *Six Guns Straight from Hell*, most recently in *Dismember the Coop: An Alice Cooper Tribute Anthology*. His plays have been produced in three countries. He also translates Korean and Indonesian into English. Bryan's translations have been published in *Asymptote* and *The Mercurian*, among others. A dead country singer (Charlie Daniels) blocked him on Twitter. He also has an inactive theatre blog at https://unknownplaywrights.wordpress.com.

Find him on Facebook and Twitter @BStubbles, though it feels like Zombie Twitter now.

Johnny Worthen is an award-winning, best-selling author of books and stories. Trained in stand-up comedy, modern literary criticism and cultural studies, he writes upmarket multi-genre fiction, symbolized by his love of tie-dye and good words. "I wear tie-dye for my friends, but I write what I like to read," he says. "This guarantees me at least one fan and easy dressing decisions in the morning."

Johnny teaches writing at the University of Utah and lives in a house with his wife, sons and assorted cats. There's also a lawn. Find him at: www.johnnyworthen.com.

Bryan Young (he/they) works across many different media. His work as a writer and producer has been called "filmmaking gold" by The New York Times. He's also published comic books with Slave Labor Graphics and Image Comics. He's been a regular contributor for the *Huffington Post*, *StarWars.com*, *Star Wars Insider magazine*, *SYFY*, */Film*, and was the founder and editor in chief of the geek news and review site *Big Shiny Robot!* In 2014, he wrote the critically acclaimed history book, ***A Children's Illustrated History of Pres-***

idential Assassination. He co-authored **Robotech: The Macross Saga RPG** and has written five books in the BattleTech Universe: **Honor's Gauntlet, A Question of Survival, Fox Tales, Without Question,** and the forthcoming **VoidBreaker.** His latest non-fiction tie-in book, **The Big Bang Theory Book of Lists** is a #1 Bestseller on Amazon. His work has won two Diamond Quill awards and in 2023 he was named Writer of the Year by the League of Utah Writers. He teaches writing for Writer's Digest, Script Magazine, and at the University of Utah. Follow him across social media @swankmotron or visit swankmotron.com.

A NOTE FROM TIMBER GHOST PRESS

If you enjoyed *This Isn't the Place: A Collection of Utah Horror*, please consider leaving a review on Amazon or Goodreads. Reviews help the authors and the press.

If you go to www.timberghostpress.com you can sign up for our newsletter so you can stay up-to-date on all our upcoming titles, plus you'll get informed of new horror flash fiction and poetry featured on our site monthly.

Take care and thanks for reading *This Isn't the Place: A Collection of Utah Horror!*

-Timber Ghost Press